A Horse Called Trouble

Jenny Hughes

A Horse
Called Trouble

A Horse Called Trouble
by
Jenny Hughes
Copyright: © 2006 by Jenny Hughes

Cover and inside illustrations: © 2006 June Brigman
Cover layout: Stabenfeldt A/S
Typeset by Roberta L. Melzl
Editor: Bobbie Chase
Printed in Germany, 2006

ISBN: 1-933343-34-6

Stabenfeldt, Inc.
457 North Main Street
Danbury, CT 06811
www.pony.us

chapter one

My room was still dark when the alarm rang, shrill and insistent. I rolled over, thumped the stop button and swung my feet to the floor, the actions blurred into one on sleep autopilot. After padding to the bathroom and splashing cold water on my face I felt a bit more awake, and as I climbed into dark jeans and a sweatshirt I saw the faintest rim of light begin to outline the closed curtains. I carried my boots downstairs, sliding my feet into them when I got outside through the back door.

It wasn't a long walk, ten minutes at most. When I reached the big house it was shrouded in a pearly mist, looking dark and shuttered. I avoided the gravel driveway, knowing how loud my crunching footsteps would sound, and moved silently along the grass edge bordering it. A quick glance toward the house's leaded windows showed me nothing, no light, no one stirring. Ducking under the top bar of a slatted wood fence I walked swiftly through a formal garden, its ornamental trees holding out stiff branches, ghostly in the gray half-light. The scent of roses, mingled softly with lavender and something I didn't recognize, followed me as the path now took me toward the first of the house's two big paddocks.

My fingertips were cold, and at first I fumbled with the gate's heavy padlock, but thanks to months of practice I soon had it open and could swing the five bar gate silently on its well-oiled hinges. The horses were three solid shadows looming before me, heads down as they grazed in companionable togetherness. Two grays, the gathering dawn picking up their light color, and the one I wanted, a chestnut gelding, well muscled under a liberal coating of mud. The lead rope was in my pocket and I slid it quickly onto the head collar he already wore. Clicking my tongue gently I took him back through the gate, relocking it firmly while he waited patiently beside me. The route out was easier, an all-weather track leading to a side exit well away from the house so I could relax and not worry so much about anyone hearing me. The lock was on the inside this time so there was no way I could refasten it, but I closed the gate firmly and led the pony away, keeping him safely against my inside shoulder.

He stepped out well, sending little flecks of mud and grass showering to the ground, and I leaned into him, breathing in his earthy, sweet smell. I wondered for the millionth time what it would be like to share this moment with a horse of my very own, and smiled when the chestnut ears flickered as the first clear notes of the birds' dawn chorus rose up to greet us. This time it was a slightly longer walk, another brisk twenty-five minutes until we reached the yard, where we turned off the road, disappearing from its view behind a row of brick built stables. Less than an hour after that first strident alarm call, and without anyone seeing or hearing me, I'd achieved what I'd set out to do.

First things first, I decided. While Merrick, the chestnut pony, greedily feasted on an energy-giving bucket of coarse mix I chomped on a banana and sorted out the stuff we both needed for the day. Merrick had obviously enjoyed a good roll the night before and only a thorough shampooing would bring his amber colored coat back to its usual shine. I'd nearly finished and was thoroughly rinsing his long, silky tail when Claudia came wandering out to join me.

"Morning, Amy," she yawned. "Did you manage to get Merrick here without disturbing your uncle?"

"Yeah, I'm an old hand at it now," I grinned, admiring the way the pale rays of the morning sun made red and gold glints sparkle in the pony's coat.

You may have been thinking you'd started reading a story by some kind of slimy horse thief, I guess, but no, I'm just your average 15-year-old girl who'd love, love, LOVE to own her own pony. My mom, who hates the title single parent but that's what she is, can't afford to buy one. Her brother, however, my Uncle George, very kindly lets me borrow Merrick, as long as I don't make a racket and wake him up when I arrive early, hence the quiet as possible creeping around. The chestnut pony used to be ridden by my cousins who have now left home, and he's supposed to be semi-retired, but he's enjoyed a new lease on life this last year with me.

We've entered every local show and Pony Club competition we could get to, and won quite a few of them too. Today was something special; a show where rival Pony Clubs compete in dressage, mounted games, mini cross-country and show jumping. The club accumulating the most points goes on to win the highly prestigious annual Cup. It was also a momentous and emotional day for me as Uncle George had decided it must be Merrick's last competition.

"He's not a youngster any more, Amy, and it's about time for him to just take things easy," he'd told me.

I was sorry, desperately sorry, because I enjoyed the shows so much. But I loved Merrick, and his welfare was the most important thing to consider. Claudia, who is our Pony Club leader, said she'd keep a sharp lookout for a loan horse of competition standard, but I knew she didn't hold out much hope. I wouldn't think about it today, I told myself, because I just wanted to make the most of the contest, have fun and do my best.

Merrick was magnificent; you'd think he knew this was his swan song. He achieved his best-ever score in the dressage, won three out of five games, and came second, with only time penalties, in the mini cross-country. Five other clubs were taking part, but the real contest was between my club and the Rangers, and at the end of the day, at the very last round of the very last class, the show jumping, the two clubs were neck and neck. Merrick and I were second to last to go, with the Rangers' top rider to follow.

We took the first few jumps perfectly, completely attuned and faster than we'd ever gone before. I was now looking at a ray of sun glinting on the daunting topmost pole of the last jump. We'd already turned toward the big upright, having achieved a textbook landing from the double followed by an immediate pickup and forward thrust. Then I felt it, the smallest stumble as Merrick faltered slightly. He'd jumped his heart out all through the class and now, at the final fence of the final round, he was doing his utmost to set an unbeatable time.

My teammates and I had it all worked out; the only way to beat the rival club was with a clear round cutting vital seconds with almost impossibly tight turns. But that stumble told me Merrick was tiring, and with a split-second decision I took him the safer route, around the outside of the ring, so our approach to the last was straight and uncomplicated. He cleared it beautifully, snapping his legs back and wasting no time in the air, but I could see disappointment on the faces turned toward us as we left the ring.

"Well done, Amy," Claudia, smiled up at me and patted Merrick's heaving shoulder. "Better to get a clear than risk knocking that last pole off."

I slid to the ground and hugged the chestnut pony, trying not to mind that the rest of the team wasn't rallying around us. To be fair they were all watching avidly as the very last rider, a brilliant competitor named Tony Welburn, hurtled around the course on his showy palomino.

"Boy, he's going fast!" I muttered and Claudia, checking her stopwatch, said tensely, "Exactly the same time as you so far. He's level coming to the second last, so –"

"He just has to cut the corner and clear it and he's won, which means his Club's won the team cup." Bitterly disappointed I turned away, burying my face in Merrick's neck, and then a huge roar from the crowd made me spin around in amazement.

"He knocked it down – they took the top pole off!" Claudia shrieked, bouncing up and down and grabbing me at the same time. "We won, Amy, we won!"

And now the rest of the team were falling on me, hugging me and patting Merrick, yelling at the tops of their lungs that we'd done the right thing to go for a clear round. I had the feeling that some of them secretly thought I'd chickened out, been too scared to whip around the corner and take the last jump at such a tight angle, but what the heck? Merrick's clear round had won the class and with it the competition and the annual Club Cup. The whole team collected the trophy and thoroughly enjoyed our lap of honor with the cheers of the crowd echoing across the show ground. As soon as we left the ring I dismounted and took Merrick's saddle off, rubbing his back vigorously to get warmth into his tired muscles.

"You're the only one doing that," a deep voice said from behind me.

I half turned my head as I continued to give the chestnut pony his massage. "Merrick's a good deal older than the other horses, so he's more likely to stiffen up."

"Ah. Was it because of his age that you didn't take that short cut to the last jump?"

I turned right around this time. "Partly. He stumbled slightly, so I knew he was getting tired."

"Good decision." The owner of the voice was tall and forty-ish with a lean, intelligent face that looked familiar.

I opened my mouth to ask who he was, and just what did it have to do with him anyway, when he strode away, moving purposefully through the crowd.

"Come on Amy," Claudia, pink and excited, darted toward

me. "They're about to make a big announcement. I didn't tell any of you before, but guess who's here today?"

I carefully covered Merrick with a light rug and followed her, bringing the gentle chestnut with me.

"Don't know. Movie star? Rock group? Or – oh!" I stopped so suddenly that Merrick bumped against the back of my arm. "Darius Caspian!"

Now it was Claudia's turn to whip around. "Who told you? No one's supposed to know."

"I just saw him," I waved my hand aimlessly. "He spoke to me."

"Darius Caspian *spoke* to you?" She made it sound like he was royalty or something, but I guess in the horse world he kind of is.

Darius, a brilliant three-day eventer in his youth, opened the Caspian Center a few years back and built up a fantastic reputation of turning out the best riders in the competitive world. Many of his former students have ridden and won at the national level, and every single one of them is not only a fantastic competitor, but also a true, dedicated horseperson of the highest caliber.

"Yeah, he came over just now. What's he *doing* here?" I caught up with her and walked alongside.

"He – oh, look there he is on the podium. He's going to announce the winner."

"Winner of what?" Puzzled, I tried to join in the applause that greeted Darius, but I was a bit muffled since I was still holding Merrick's reins.

"Thank you," the deep voice echoed through the show grounds' loudspeakers. "I'll start by saying how much I've enjoyed watching today's competition. The standard of riding was very high, and every single one of you should be proud."

Most of us tried to look suitably modest, but I noticed several excited members of our winning Pony Club doing high fives and making victory salutes.

"I'm here," Darius continued. "Because this year a special scholarship prize has been set up, to be awarded by me at meetings such as this, all around the country. Each recipient, the rider I deem most eligible, wins a month's stay at the Caspian Center, with full tuition."

There was a big intake of breath, a sort of mass 'aaah,' and a real electric buzz hummed through the crowd. OK, so you might be thinking *Big deal*, because you were expecting the prize to be a trip to Disneyland or something, but believe me, we all thought this was a million times better. Dreamily I stroked Merrick's soft nose and tried to imagine what the month would be like. I guessed someone like Tony Welburn and his talented golden horse would win and they'd have this fantastic time and come back better and faster than ever. Vaguely, through my daydream, I heard someone say my name so I blinked and looked around. Everyone, and I mean *everyone*, was staring at me, open mouthed and stunned-looking.

"Oh Amy, wow!" Claudia said softly and I gaped at her dumbly.

"Wow what?"

"You've won, you big dork. You're going to the Caspian Center!" She practically fell on me. "I'm so proud!"

Suddenly the crowd erupted and everyone who knew me rushed over and started slapping me on the back, yelling and hollering and whoop-whooping. It was sheer chaos, and even calm old Merrick showed the whites of his eyes and started shuffling nervously. I didn't know what to do. I was completely in shock, and Claudia came quickly to my rescue.

"You go and talk to Darius and I'll deal with your horse."

She led Merrick away to a quiet spot while I started staggering toward the podium in a complete daze. The crowd parted good-humoredly for me and I got a lot of friendly 'well dones' and 'congratulations,' but as I ducked under a rope a sneering voice said, "It's all a big fix, if you ask me."

"Fix?" I looked straight into the furious face of Tony Welburn. "Why d'you say that?"

"Because this award is meant for the best rider, and you're not it."

"Oh, get lost." I can't stand bad losers. "My horse did great, and you know it."

"He's an old donkey and he's not even yours," Tony was in a really foul mood. "You chickened out in that last round and it was sheer bad luck that I just touched the pole."

"No, it was sheer bad judgment," Darius's deep voice held a new edge. "You cut it too fine and gave your pony too much to do. Amy's not chicken, just a far more considerate and talented rider. That's why I chose her."

I could see a dark, angry flush flooding Tony's sneering face and waited for his well-known temper to explode, but there was something in the way Darius held his gaze that made Tony drop his eyes and turn away. I think that was the moment I started developing a serious case of hero worship – the man was just so cool!

"So Amy, are you pleased you won?" His dark eyes had

14

lighter flecks in them that shone with a warm glow when he spoke to me.

Don't get me wrong, I certainly didn't have a crush on him or anything gross like that – he's as old as my friends' dads – but he was *awesome*.

"I really am," I took a deep breath. "But Tony was right about one thing. I don't have a horse. Merrick belongs to my uncle."

"No problem," Darius grinned, looking totally different from the steely-eyed guy who'd taken Tony away. "None of the winners gets to bring their ponies. You'll all be riding mine."

This was just getting better and better. I walked alongside the great Darius Caspian as he explained his ideas for our training. Deeply engrossed, I hardly noticed a tall figure approaching until Darius said, "Oh hi. Amy, I'd like you to meet Matt, the rider I picked from the Southwest Area. In a few weeks you two will be spending a lot of time together."

I looked up and felt my insides perform some kind of triple salsa. Matt was about 16, six feet of blue-eyed blonde handsomeness, and he was smiling in obvious admiration straight into my eyes. I'd thought nothing could make the prize I'd just won any more exciting, but oh boy, Matt looked as if he might be the gorgeous icing on the Caspian Center cake!

chapter two

By the time I led Merrick back to his field I was exhausted, though still on Cloud Nine. I often kept his bridle on after a day out and rode him bareback from Claudia's yard to Uncle George's, but the chestnut pony must have been a lot more tired than I was, so I walked beside him instead. He got an extra yummy feed and about a hundred cuddles before I left.

"Remember, it's not goodbye. I'll come over and see you, maybe even ride you sometimes, but today was the last of our shows together." I gave him one last kiss and released him into his field, smiling ruefully as he ignored me completely and trotted back to his friends.

The short walk home seemed to take twice as long as it had in the morning and I reached the gate just as my mom's car drew up and she leaped out.

"How did you do? Did your Club win the Cup?" She was still dressed in her stylish work clothes and was unloading groceries she'd bought on the way home.

"Yeah we did. Merrick was terrific." Wearily I picked up a grocery bag and followed her in.

"Oh well done, Amy," she plunked the groceries down and gave me a hug. "I'm really sorry I couldn't be there."

"It's OK. Mom, guess what? Not only did the Club get the Team Cup, but I won a special prize."

"No!" She kicked off her high-heeled office shoes and was immediately shorter than I.

Teasingly I patted the top of her head and told her about the Caspian Center.

"But Amy," she said worriedly. "How can you do it without a pony? George was adamant about Merrick retiring."

"It's fine. Darius is letting us ride his own horses. I've got all the details, but can I have a bath before I show you? I'm exhausted."

"I bet you are. I heard you leave, and it felt like the middle of the night. I'm guessing none of the other Pony Club kids get up as early as you."

"That's because they don't have to catch their horse out in a field, and then walk him to Claudia's and wash the mud off before they start getting ready for the show," I explained patiently and her eager face fell.

"I'm sorry we can't afford to buy you your own. If you find a good loan horse I can manage to pay for his keep and all that. It's just –"

"I know, Mom, it's all right, don't worry."

My dad left before I was born, and it's been a struggle for her financially.

"I mean," she *was* worrying. "I could ask George to help, but –"

"But you don't want to and why should you?" I knew my

17

uncle, though basically kind at heart, was pretty tight with money and, to be honest, a bit of an all-around misery. "Something will turn up, and I do have this amazing working vacation with Darius Caspian to look forward to."

She wrinkled her nose. "Another month of getting up at the crack of dawn and working horses all day. Not my idea of a vacation."

"But definitely mine," I stowed some of the groceries in a cupboard and went for a long, long soak in the bathtub.

Lying up to my ears in warm bubbles I heard Mom call out, "Amy, phone!" but couldn't be bothered to haul myself out. When I eventually got downstairs she had changed into sweat pants and was padding around comfortably barefoot as she prepared my favorite pasta dish for supper.

"So," she raised her eyebrows and pretended to look severe. "Who's Matt? Is there something you haven't told me about today, Amy Weston?"

I felt my freshly washed face glow like a lamp and tried to keep my voice casual. "He's just some guy who won the Caspian Center prize for the Southwest area. Why?"

"Why, she says. That was he on the phone, that's why. How did he get your number?"

"Oh, um, he said we might want to talk before we meet up again. What did he say, and – oh what did you say, Mom? Please tell me it was nothing embarrassing!"

"As if. He said he'd call back, and I think he will. He sounded eager, so you must have made quite an impression."

Inwardly I berated myself for not getting out of the bathtub, and told myself Mom probably had it all wrong; he wasn't eager at all and wouldn't phone again – ever. She was right, though. In fact he called before we'd even

18

finished our pasta, and he kept on phoning three or four times a week for the next month. It was great that he did. I really felt I was getting to know him and it made the waiting for what Mom had written on the calendar – CASPIAN CENTER DAY!!!! – a lot more bearable.

When I'd finally stuffed the very last T-shirt I could squeeze into my backpack and checked for the umpteenth time that all my riding gear was carefully stowed away in a separate suitcase, I could hardly speak for excitement. Mom hadn't been able to get the day off from work, but had promised she'd drive up in a month for our final day, so I was catching an early bus. It was full of shoppers and people visiting relatives, and I felt highly privileged to be the only one heading off for the experience of a lifetime.

I was nervous, though, and really, *really* glad to find Matt already at the Center waiting for me. He was even better looking than I remembered and I felt my knees buckle slightly when he leaned forward to take my bag.

"I've only been here about 20 minutes," he told me. "So all I've done is throw my stuff in my room, but from what I've seen it's quite a place!"

He wasn't wrong – the Caspian Center looked every bit as elegant and well organized as I'd imagined. The Pony Club winners were staying in the modern wing of what I guess was the original house, a lovely old, ivy-covered, stone building. Our wing was plainer and more functional, probably built expressly for Caspian students. Margo, a really nice, motherly lady who introduced herself as the 'housekeeper slash Dear Abby,' took me up to see my room, which was small but OK and had a view across a lush paddock where, in the distance, several horses grazed.

19

"The official tour's not until everyone else gets here," Matt told me. "So, d'you want to chill and hang around the house, or –"

"I'd rather go and see the stables, if we're allowed," I said immediately. "I can't wait to meet the horses."

He grinned, teeth very white in his tanned face. "Awesome. We can check them over and pick out the best two before the other prize winners arrive."

"Yeah, right. I can just see Darius letting us get away with that!" I laughed.

We headed outside to find the stable yard, four immaculate rows of stalls arranged in a square bordering a quadrangle.

"This is great," Matt shoved his hands in his jeans pockets. "I like the way the horses can look over their doors at each other and everything that's going on in the yard."

"Yeah," I agreed. "If there were any horses *here*, of course."

To my disappointment the stables were completely vacant, bedding cleared, floors washed, hayracks and water buckets empty.

"They're all turned out. Today's day off day," a smiling, plump pretty girl walked toward us. "Ooh, I said day three times, but at least I made it clear. I'm Tracey, Caspian Center groom. You must be Pony Club winners."

"I'm Amy, this is Matt," we shook hands self-consciously and I noticed Tracey took off her glasses to smile at the handsome Matt.

"The ponies your group will be riding are through there," she pointed to where a gap showed in one of the lines of stalls.

"Thanks, Tracey," Matt and I started walking toward the

gap which proved to be a wide, paved track leading straight to the paddock I'd seen from my window.

There were eight ponies in the big field facing us, dotted around in groups of two or three, except for one lone bay at the very far end. We climbed over the gate and moved quietly toward the first group, a dapple-gray and two chestnuts. They seemed pretty happy to see us and enjoyed some petting and sweet talk from me, and some macho patting and 'nice type' remarks from Matt. Two bays were next, one light colored, one dark, and they also welcomed us in friendly fashion. An enormous black gelding and a lightly built gray came over to see what was going on, and as we were introducing ourselves to them Matt looked up and saw Tracey waving at us.

"Some of the others have just arrived," she yelled. "Do you want to come and say hello?"

"Sure," Matt started walking back toward the gate immediately, but I hung back.

The one horse we hadn't met, the solitary bay at the furthest end of the paddock, had made no move to come over and I felt sorry for him, seemingly excluded from the rest of the herd as he was.

"I'll catch up," I called to Matt. "I just want to check out this last pony."

Matt hesitated, but I guess he thought he'd have looked like a real nerd in front of Tracey if he'd turned back and trotted after me, so he said, "OK, don't be long," and kept going.

As I approached the bay horse he looked up from his grazing briefly and seemed to size me up before moving deliberately away. Twice more I tried to get near him, but

21

although he didn't run he made it perfectly clear that he didn't want me around, thanks very much. Merrick had always been the easiest pony in the world to catch so I didn't have any experience to draw on, but I thought maybe this solitary horse was the equine equivalent of shy and preferred to be the one who made the first move. So I sat down and waited.

At first he seemed quite content to keep on ignoring me, but when I made no attempt to go after him but simply stayed where I was, cross-legged on the ground, he began to get interested. I talked to him quietly, not commands or entreaties, just trivial nonsense really, but he seemed to like the sound of my voice and gradually got a little closer. After ten minutes or so he was beside me, looking down curiously while I kept on telling him about my day's journey. When he dropped his nose to sniff my hair I took it to be a sign he'd welcome a little contact so I carefully got to my feet, keeping my hands still and my voice calm, and let him run his sensitive lips along my arm. He was beautiful close up, a fine head with intelligent dark eyes, deep chest, strong neck and clean, perfect legs. Bay is never the showiest color but his coat shone with good health and grooming, and the black mane and tail were thick and glossy.

"You are a stunner," I told him, still letting him do all the touchy-feely stuff. "In a quiet way, of course, and I think you have a personality to match. You're just not interested in showing it, are you?"

He snorted gently and I breathed in the sweet, gloriously horsey smell of him. We were both standing quite still, noses touching, and I felt an enormous sense of connection, a great welling surge of emotion that's impossible to describe.

Breathing out as he was breathing in, I moved my hand for the first time, stroking his shoulder in a gentle, rhythmic motion. Fifteen minutes later he was stretching his neck and nodding contentedly as if to say 'don't stop.' I'd quite happily have stayed there for hours getting to know him, but from across the gate end of the field a faint voice was yelling my name. I knew it was Matt and hoped he'd have the sense to stay away, but when the bay horse jerked his head sharply and turned to look across the paddock I realized our bonding session was over.

"I gotta go," I told him. "But I'll be back, and if we *are* allowed to choose which horse, you know I'll pick you."

"You've been here for ages. What are you doing?" Matt sounded quite irritable as I watched the bay pony move unhurriedly away.

"Nothing," I was annoyed too, wishing he'd had the sensitivity to leave us alone. "What do you want?"

"Uh –" poor Matt looked alarmed at my tone, not knowing what he'd done wrong. "You said you were coming in to meet the others."

"OK," I started walking beside him, swallowing my irritation. "What are they like?"

"One girl still hasn't arrived, but the other one, Kelly, seems nice. The two guys are Jack, he's about fifteen, and Liam who's one of those in-your-face types."

"I take it you weren't too crazy about Liam?" I turned and smiled at him.

He grinned back immediately, looking relieved that I'd stopped being cold to him. "Oh he'll probably calm down. A lot of people go overboard when they first meet you."

I saw what he meant as soon as we went into the house.

24

Kelly, a petite redhead, greeted me in suitably friendly fashion, and ditto Jack, but Liam, who was your classic tall, dark and handsome, bounced across the room and nearly knocked me over.

"Hi, Amy! Hey Matt, you didn't tell us your girlfriend was such a babe! I'm Liam, nearly seventeen and free as a bird, but you could change that."

Cheesy line, or what!

"Thanks," I said dryly. "But I was thinking more of concentrating on my riding skills. Probably a good idea, since we're at the Caspian Center, don'tcha think?"

"Feisty as well as fabulous!" He really was way too much. "You're a lucky man, Matt. Hey, is that a taxi pulling up out there? Could be Number Six arriving."

He hurtled out of the room leaving the rest of us blinking slightly.

"I didn't say you were my girlfriend," Matt hissed uncomfortably. "Just told him we'd met once and spoken on the phone."

"Don't worry about it. As you said, he's bound to calm down."

"We can only hope," Kelly said fervently and Jack laughed.

The four of us were making that slightly awkward, polite small talk you do on such occasions when the door opened again and Liam, a totally astonished Liam, stood holding an enormous suitcase.

"Um – guys, this is Paris Lombard, winner of the Midwest prize."

A vision in pink designer wear stepped forward, the long, silky curtain of her hair rippling in a blonde stream almost to her waist. Everything about her, face, nails and figure,

25

was absolutely perfect, and I could see Matt and Jack join Liam immediately in a kind of stunned trance.

"Hello," I said, hoping I didn't look at all intimidated. "Nice to meet you."

"Yeah, you too," her voice, shrill and petulant, was a let-down. "I'm shattered, totally shattered. Is this place the back of beyond or what? I thought the cab driver had gotten lost. I should have insisted on my Dad chartering a plane, but that'll teach me!"

"P – plane?" Kelly stuttered.

"Oh sure, honey, we do it all the time," she sat down and crossed her elegant legs. "Is there tea or something? Liam, sweetie you ought to take my case upstairs so they can unpack."

"We actually do our own unpacking," I said quickly, not wanting her to start demanding Margo do it. "And in fact I haven't done my own yet, so I'll come up with you if you like."

"Yeah, me too," Kelly had recovered her cool and winked cheekily at the three catatonic guys. "We'll leave you boys to talk. I'm betting you'll have plenty to say!"

chapter three

Kelly and I helped Paris lug the huge suitcase up the stairs and along the corridor to her room.

"You – um – have a lot of clothes," I offered lamely, thinking of my modest backpack and bag.

"Yeah I do, but where the heck I'm supposed to wear them around this dump I don't know," her moaning was already beginning to get on my nerves and Kelly obviously felt the same.

"Why did you come then?" she asked bluntly, pushing open a bedroom door. "You didn't have to accept, and most Pony Clubbers would give their right arm for a month here."

"Yeah well, I was determined to do the competitive training, but maybe I should have booked a good hotel for the duration," the beautiful blonde sniffed as she surveyed her room. "This is more like a prison cell, if you ask me."

"It's fine," I said peaceably. "Anyway, you'll only be sleeping in here, after all."

"Mm," she didn't appear mollified. "Dad said I'd have to rough it if I wanted to be taught by Darius Caspian, and I guess he was right. Oh well," she kicked off impossibly gorgeous shoes. "Give me a call when supper's ready, will you girls? I'm going to take a shower and a nap."

She swung the door shut practically in our faces and Kelly and I gaped at each other for a moment. Then I started giggling and she joined in, making me laugh even more until we were rolling around the corridor in complete hysterics.

"She's – she's like a cross between a Barbie doll and a werewolf," Kelly spluttered. "And we've got a whole month of her!"

"Nah," I tried to pull myself together. "From what I saw of Darius he won't stand for any of her nonsense, so she'll probably be out of here in the first available taxi."

"Or private jet!" Kelly set us off again, and by the time we'd unpacked our stuff and hung out of each other's window to compare views we were on really good terms.

By the time we went back downstairs Matt and Jack seemed to be getting along well too, and the four of us had a lively pinball competition, which helped break the ice further.

"Glad to see you're all settling in." Darius's familiar, deep voice held the slightest trace of an accent, I noticed. "Where are Paris and Liam?"

"She's in her room," I said tactfully. "And we don't know where Liam went."

"Probably outside sizing up the horses," Darius said. "Anyone else had a look?"

I opened my mouth to say yes I had, and please could I

ride the lonely bay pony when Paris made another of her entrances. She'd changed all her clothes and was now dressed entirely in white, wafting into the room in a cloud of heavenly perfume.

"Darius," she put out a slender hand. "Lovely to see you, but I'm afraid the room won't do. It's far too small and has a view of some kind of shed."

Darius raised a satanic-looking eyebrow. "It's a barn. If you don't like it don't look out the window."

Her mouth dropped open. "But –"

"No buts, Paris. Dinner's in ten minutes and I'll see you all in the lecture room in the new wing in an hour," he turned on his heel, leaving her still gaping.

"Well!"

Fearing another of her outbursts the rest of us started jabbering at once, and it wasn't until Liam joined us that Paris got any more attention. He'd gotten over the first knock-out impact she had made and was now flirting outrageously with her, making her giggle and toss her hair around a lot. At least it stopped her moaning about everything and, feeling thankful for that, I smiled gratefully at Liam. He immediately winked back and blew me a kiss behind her back, which caused Matt to make a funny growling noise in his throat and glare angrily at the two of us. All in all I was relieved when we went in to eat, and found myself hoping that the riding training, when it started, would be so all-consuming the six of us would be too tired for all these soap opera complications.

The regime started right after our meal with an introductory talk by Darius. He started by welcoming us all and said we'd be getting a full tour of inspection so we knew where everything was when the actual course began the next morning. Then came a brief explanation of his methods.

"You're all good riders, exceptionally good in some cases, so physically there aren't a lot of changes to be made. What I do want to work on is your mental attitude and intelligent approach. Instead of riding the horses you know well and have won on many times, you'll be riding unknown quantities from my own stock. These are all properly schooled and capable of doing everything you ask them, but I want you to see each one as an individual, using his strengths and weaknesses to get the best results from each exercise. Any questions?"

I raised my hand slightly diffidently. "Do we get to choose the horse we ride?"

"No – well, on a couple of occasions, but I'll tell you more about those later. Generally the horses will be randomly selected and, as I say, it's up to you to read each one, discover his quirks and dislikes as well as his positive attributes."

"How long will we have to do that?" Jack asked.

"It will vary. Sometimes during a warm-up for a class or the hour before a session, sometimes only the few seconds you ride him into the competitive ring."

There was an audible intake of breath as the six of us digested this extraordinary concept. I thought Paris would have a million questions and objections but she stayed surprisingly quiet while the extrovert Liam looked as though he was already relishing the prospect.

"He's very confident," I remarked to Matt, but he only grunted and wouldn't make eye contact so I knew I was still off his favorites list.

The tour was mind-boggling. You name it, the Caspian

Center had it: indoor ring, outdoor rings, fabulous jumping rings, cross country courses, plus the paddocks, outbuildings, house and stable yard. It was obviously a huge commercial enterprise, and I wondered why at the moment the only guests were half a dozen Pony Clubbers.

Darius touched on the subject as he concluded the tour. "The prize you all won is very much an experimental venture, and this year I want to concentrate on it. Apart from a few horses for re-schooling your group will be getting my full attention."

I just couldn't wait, and would have loved to share my excitement with Matt, but even after the tour he was still huffy and uncommunicative. He wouldn't join in with another pinball game, but just sat sulkily watching a movie on TV while next to him Liam and Paris flirted with each other as if it were an Olympic sport and they were leading competitors. I wondered miserably if Matt secretly liked Paris himself, but told myself firmly I was not going down that jealousy road. Matt and I had gotten along fabulously over the phone in the last few weeks, but it's different when you're actually with someone, so although I was disappointed he didn't seem to like me now I just had to accept it. Anyway, I really wanted to concentrate on getting the most out of the Caspian experience, so after a hurried breakfast next morning, when Matt was polite but distant, Paris and Liam were glued to each other and Kelly and Jack were just normal, I couldn't wait to go out to the yard. To my surprise it was still empty.

"Morning, guys," Tracey walked toward us with an armful of head collars. "First you get to catch your horse, and then you bring him in, groom and tack him up."

"You're kidding!" Paris looked horrified. "I don't do all that. I have a groom."

Tracey handed her a head collar. "Not here, you don't."

"Can we choose which pony?" I was already moving toward the paddock.

"I'd grab the nearest one," she replied practically, but I ignored that, having already spotted the bay horse way across the field on his own again.

"What are their names?" Matt asked, coiling up his lead rope in a professional looking way.

"Um," Tracey, put her glasses back on briefly to look into the field. "The two chestnuts are Krona and Shula; gray, Baily; light bay, Fallon; dapple, Triest; black, Shaft; and dark bay, Rogan. Say, where are you going, Amy?"

"Over there," I pointed to the lone bay away from the group of seven. "I want that one."

She shrugged. "I wouldn't, but I'm not supposed to influence any of you."

I hardly listened, but just kept walking fast. "Oh," I half-turned. "What's *his* name?"

"Trouble," she was watching Paris fumble as she tried to slip a rope around Fallon's neck. "That one's a horse called Trouble."

'Awful name,' I thought but I didn't care and I wasn't going to worry about the other hints she'd dropped. I was soon approaching the solitary bay, hoping he'd remember me and the magical way we'd seemed to connect. He raised his head and regarded me solemnly, and then moved deliberately away.

"Aw, come on, boy. Come on, Trouble!" I used my best coaxing voice and didn't chase after him. "It's me, Amy."

He stopped a few yards away and looked at me. Although I knew we had to have the horses clean, saddled, and ready in half an hour I still didn't make a move toward him, but just stood very quietly and talked soothingly. It seemed like ages, but in fact it was only a few minutes before the bay pony strolled casually in my direction until he was near enough to touch. I didn't, though, and kept my hands, especially the one holding the head collar, very still until he took another step and nudged me gently with his nose. Now I raised my hand and tickled behind his ears, telling him how clever and beautiful he was, and I kept up the stream of inane compliments all the while I was buckling up the head collar and leading him back across the field. The other five students had all gone, of course, leaving one chestnut and the dapple-gray pony, who'd returned to their grazing.

Tracey was still at the gate and she grinned broadly and gave me a thumbs up. "Well done! He can be an absolute devil to catch sometimes."

"Is that why he's called Trouble?" I patted the bay lovingly.

She laughed as she polished her glasses and put them back on. "Sorry. That's just a lame joke. Darius once said that's what he should be called, and I thought it was funny. His real name is Rory."

"Oh that's better, isn't it Rory? Come on, we'd better start grooming you."

"You'll soon catch up with Paris, at any rate," Tracey was evidently a bit of a gossip. "She doesn't know one brush from another, so the handsome dark guy said he'd help her when he's finished his."

"Handsome – oh, you mean Liam," I was admiring the way Rory walked.

"Yeah. Are they an item, those two?"

"They only met yesterday," I said cautiously and smiled to myself when Tracey quickly whipped off her glasses again as she went to talk to Liam.

I led Rory into an empty stable and started to work on removing the dried mud and dust from his coat. He really did seem to like the sound of my voice so I kept on talking as I worked and found that, although sensitive and ticklish in a couple of spots, he was an absolute pleasure to groom. The thought of riding him filled me with incredible excitement, and when the moment came and I sprang lightly into the saddle I had such a soppy, delighted grin on my face that even the gloomy Matt half-smiled back at me. One of Rory's sensitive skin areas was under the very edge of the saddlecloth, so I took care not to put too much pressure there and was delighted with the responsive way he moved for me during our fifteen-minute warm-up period. Unfortunately our burgeoning partnership didn't last long.

We followed Tracey to a big, flat field where markers, hurdles and poles had been laid to neatly define several different areas. There were several people with clipboards and stopwatches, who were soon joined by Darius.

"Hi again," he was shuffling some papers. "I've got an interesting exercise to get you started. The six of you have brought along a horse each and I want you to dismount and stand beside him." When we'd done so, he looked us over intently. "Right. We have Paris with Baily, Matt with Fallon, Jack with Shula, Kelly with Shaft, Amy with Rory and Liam with Rogan. Out there," he pointed, "are six numbered areas of different disciplines, and I'll be handing each of you an individual checklist."

I thought I was following the plot so far, but there were already a few blank faces.

"For instance, on Matt's checklist he must ride Rogan to area 3 which contains three small jumps. Matt must clear all three within the prescribed time and an official will record his score. He then rides out of 3, finds Shula and rides her to area 1, the dressage ring, where they'll perform a test called out and marked by the judge. Meanwhile," he looked at another paper. "Kelly will be riding Fallon to area 6 where they'll negotiate a line of bending poles before Kelly takes Baily to area 2, and so on and so on."

I blinked and hoped the whole thing would be a lot clearer when we actually started doing it. We were given only a few minutes to digest the rules, look to see where each numbered area was and go through the names of the horses before we were handed our checklists. They were brief and to the point. Mine read; Baily 1, Rogan 4, Shula 2, Rory 3, Shaft 5, Fallon 6.

"Ready?" Darius seemed not to notice the dismay on most of our faces.

"Sure thing," Liam said confidently.

"On your marks then, get set, GO!" Darius clicked his stopwatch and stepped back.

For a split second no one moved, but then Liam marched over and took hold of Shula's reins, so I shook myself and turned to get the gray, Baily, from Paris, who gaped at me helplessly when I handed her Rory.

"But I don't want him. I have to start with Shaft!" she wailed.

"So go get him!" I hissed back, swinging into Baily's saddle and heading for area 1 at a brisk trot.

The gray pony was also very responsive, and when I asked for canter I gasped at the instant speed he produced. He wasn't so interested in stopping, I found, and I had to concentrate hard on keeping the pace under control as we cantered 10 and 20 yard circles, trotted the center line and did everything else called out to us. Baily's brakes were definitely his weak point, so I resisted the urge to gallop flat out across the field to my next horse, the dark bay, Rogan. Although almost identical in color to Rory I thought Rogan was easy to identify, being of slightly heavier build and lacking the fine, handsome head of my favorite. Though very fast, he was easier to handle than Baily, stopping immediately when I asked, so I could tell he had a much more sensitive mouth.

The Number 4 area contained trotting poles, often despised by riders who regularly jump fairly high fences, but I knew their value, both to horse and rider, and entered the ring confidently at a rhythmic rising trot. The groups of poles were set in a flowing serpentine with central ones on the diagonal, and I was told by the official to complete the course on the right rein, and then the left. Rogan's natural eye and well-developed muscles were a great help, and he seemed happy with the light, steady contact I kept throughout. From the corner of my eye I saw the official check his watch and write something down, but I was already cantering out of the ring, scanning the big field to find the chestnut, Shula. She was way over on the other side, and before I could reach her Jack came charging toward me on Fallon.

"Amy, I need Rogan, quick!" He launched himself off the light bay's back and grabbed at my reins.

"OK," I dismounted, we swapped horses and flew off in opposite directions, with me still heading for Shula and Jack hurtling off on his own course.

I know what you're thinking – the whole thing sounds completely, absolutely, raving mad, and I must say that even while I was doing it I was in complete agreement with you!

chapter four

It was wonderful, wonderful fun, and I loved the way that, despite the chaos, we were expected to show how quick-witted and adaptable we were. Shula, my next horse, gave me a gentle reminder. She was just leaving area 6, and as I needed her in area 2 I barely had time to say hello before we were galloping like the wind across the big expanse of springy grass. The chestnut mare responded as though she was having a ball and gave some excited little bucks as we were approaching ring 2.

Entering it I gave an inward groan when I was instructed to begin some lateral flatwork. It's not what I'm best at, and Shula was so over-excited there was no way I was going to get her to concentrate. I spent a few quiet minutes calming her down to improve her focus, figuring it was better to get time faults than mess up the exercises completely. My soothing approach seemed to do the trick, and to my surprise the flighty chestnut was very clever, ending the routine with a foot-perfect pirouette at canter.

"I've never managed that before, Shula," I told her as we left the ring. "So thanks very much."

My spirits lifted even more as I headed off to get Rory and take him to area number 3, which contained three medium-sized fences. Rory, who'd just been ridden by Liam, had his ears back and was looking distinctly unsettled, so instead of charging straight over to the jumps again I took a little time out. For Rory it was a short session of sweet-talk, using the soothing nonsense phrases he seemed to like so much. He responded well, stopped tossing his head up and down and stood beautifully as I climbed gently into his saddle. I'd gotten the feel of him on our warm-up, and rode him positively but with the light leg contact he preferred.

We were timed from the instant we entered ring 3. I approached the first fence, a simple staircase, at a buoyant, well-balanced canter to clear it easily, with a smooth curve to the second and another perfect take-off and landing. I took every care not to lose my balance and jolt the sensitive Rory in any way. The third and final jump was a parallel set at an angle, but it presented no problems, and I felt a glorious sense of elation, another feeling of oneness with the talented bay pony as he cleared it in perfect style.

I almost wanted to stop right then and there, but Darius had choreographed the exercise, and of course I had to complete it, so we set off across the field to get Shaft. The big black horse looked as though he was enjoying himself too, and seemed very easy and uncomplicated to ride, but I soon realized he was naturally a bit clumsy, and groaned inwardly when I saw the obstacle course we had to maneuver in the next ring. Shaft hopped over a couple of hay bales and stood obligingly still while I fished around in a bucket of water for an apple. He didn't object at all to wearing a veil when we did the dress up bit, but he stumbled through the tires-on-the-ground and barged right through the gate we were supposed to open first.

"Sorry, pal, my fault," I patted him kindly as we set off for my last horse, Fallon, and area 6.

I was concentrating so hard I had no idea how anyone else was doing, but as Shaft and I passed number 3 I briefly saw Paris finishing the jump course with Baily. To my absolute amazement the girl was a revelation, the most perfectly balanced rider I had ever seen, and the gray horse was responding beautifully. I knew Paris had to be a prizewinner, obviously, or she wouldn't be here, but I just hadn't expected her to be so talented. Still, there wasn't time to give it much thought – I had one last horse to get and the last area to discover.

As I continued crossing the field I could hear Paris and Liam begin a humungous argument across one of the rings, screaming their heads off at one another. Glad I wasn't involved, I waited outside area 2 for Fallon, who was doing lateral work with Matt. The light bay horse was performing faultlessly and I gave Matt a reserved 'well done' as I took the reins. Matt gave me his fabulous grin, a bit reluctant but it had *that* glow to it, and I rode off for my last effort with a lovely soppy-happy feeling. I cantered Fallon into the ring and approached a set of bending poles, set in a long, straight line. I *love* bending races, and the pony I was riding must have felt the same, snaking his way through the poles in what had to be a record breaking time. I patted

him a lot, told him he was amazing, and left the ring to gallop back to the start.

I could see Matt racing just ahead of me, and was thrilled to be the second to arrive. Although I knew this didn't mean I was automatically in the first three because all the scores had yet to be added up, I still felt a great surge of elation and wished I was riding Rory so I could hug him. Soon after, Kelly came thundering up, closely followed by Jack, but it was several minutes before Paris joined us.

"Honestly, that Liam!" she was all pink and flustered. "I made a mistake, I admit it, but you'd think I'd tried to murder him or something."

"Murder?" Kelly raised her eyebrows. "What did you do wrong?"

"Liam wanted whatsisname – Rogan – for his last thing, but I had the blasted horse thinking he was Rory," Paris stopped and glared at us. "Don't laugh! It's a mistake anyone could make. They look exactly the same."

"No they don't," I said instantly. "Rory's head is much finer."

"Well, aren't you the clever one, Amy?" Paris's voice was shriller than ever. "So, OK, maybe I'm the only person here dumb enough to ride the same horse twice, but that's what I did."

"How did Liam react?" Kelly wanted to know.

"You know how he reacted. You must have heard him! I was doing the obstacle course and Liam was yelling I had the wrong horse and to come out because he should be riding Rogan."

"What did you do?" Jack was still trying not to laugh.

"I ignored him, of course," she said loftily. "He had to

wait until I finished, and he went absolutely ballistic. Called me horrible names and everything."

"Horrible? I haven't even started yet. You made me lose this contest, you stupid dork!" Liam, his good-looking face contorted with rage, tugged hard on Rogan's soft mouth to make him stand.

"Hey!" I shouted. "Call each other what you like, but don't take your temper out on the horse, Liam!"

"You can shut up, too," he turned furiously, and Matt immediately rode between us.

"Leave Amy alone and stop acting like a big kid. You'll get kicked out if Darius sees you."

Liam controlled himself with difficulty and rode away, followed by Paris who was still nagging and whining at him.

"If ever two people deserved each other, it's those two," Jack said fervently and Kelly laughed as they both turned their horses to go back to the yard.

"Are you OK?" Matt looked into my eyes and I felt everything bounce around in my insides.

"Oh yeah," I said, trying to sound casual, then, in case I'd been *too* casual, added, "Thanks for setting Liam straight. He was totally out of line, wasn't he?"

"He sure was. I guess he's not the complete charmer you girls seemed to think."

I shrugged, about to reply that I didn't find Liam particularly charming, but decided against starting an argument. "How did you make out this morning?"

Matt seemed to like the change of subject. "I enjoyed myself, but I was floundering a bit. I don't know about you, but by the time I got the right horse and found the right area I was completely psyched. Everything we were asked to do was really easy. I've done more complicated dressage and much bigger jumping courses and so on, but what with getting adjusted to a different horse each time I found the whole thing – I don't know – challenging, I guess."

"Challenging is a good word for it," I gave Fallon a long rein so he could stretch his neck on the cooling down walk. "I was amazed that I didn't finish way slower than everyone else because twice I took extra time to calm the horse down before we went into the ring."

"I wish I'd done that. I practically flattened the bending poles rushing Shaft straight at them."

I laughed, but with him, not at him. "I did the same with him on the obstacle course. He's a sweetie-pie, but not built for mounted games, I'd say."

"I wasted the most time rounding up the horses I needed to ride," Matt said ruefully. "Somehow I never managed to keep an eye on where everyone was, and I spent half the time riding horses I didn't want, and then hanging around waiting for the ones I did want."

"I was lucky. I didn't have to do much of that." I patted Fallon. "Though I'd have liked to ride Rory back. He jumped beautifully for me, and I can't think why they nicknamed him Trouble."

"I can," Matt said ruefully. "He can be an absolute devil! Talented and quick and all that, but if you don't please him he just won't cooperate. I think everyone else had a real problem with him. In fact I wouldn't be surprised if Paris deliberately avoided riding him and just pretended to mistake Rogan for him."

"No way," I said firmly. "If anyone could handle him it would be Paris. She's the best rider I've ever seen."

"You're joking!" Matt looked genuinely amazed at the thought. "I didn't get to watch her, though I saw both Kelly and Jack while I was waiting to pick up a horse. They're pretty good, too."

"It seems we're a talented group, doesn't it?" I grinned at him, and when he smiled back I was glad it was the sort of look that made my knees buckle.

When we got back to the yard everyone was busy untacking and brushing down their horses. I enjoyed doing Fallon, but once he was settled I ran over to the stable where Rory was pulling quietly at a hay net.

"Hello, baby," I crooned and was thrilled when he gave me a small nicker of greeting. I slipped into the stall and spent another half hour with him, just renewing acquaintance and rubbing his velvety ears the way he liked.

"Who's in there?" Tracey, glasses flashing in the sun, put her head over the door.

"It's me, Amy," I said. "Is it OK to do this?"

"You're due in the lecture room in three minutes, but sure. You've taken quite a shine to our troublesome boy, haven't you?"

"He's gorgeous," I gave Rory one last cuddle and left the stable, almost barreling into Liam, who'd appeared from nowhere.

"Hello, Liam," Tracey could whip those specs off quicker than anyone I knew. "How did you do?"

"Don't ask," he said shortly. "I got sabotaged."

I made no comment and went to move past him, but he caught my arm.

"Amy, I'm sorry I bawled you out. You were right to tell me I was being rough on the horse."

46

"Glad you realize it."

"I do," he fell into step alongside me. "I went for a walk to cool off and I've been back to check Rogan over again and apologize to him, too."

"How did he take that?" I asked dryly.

"Totally fine. He's a terrific pony – said 'no hard feelings and thanks for the apple!'" Liam put on a silly high-pitched voice.

He sounded very funny and I laughed and said lightly that I'd forgive him too. "And I bet Paris will be OK when she calms down."

His good-looking face darkened. "You think? My opinion is she's a 10 carat genu-INE witch, and I'm going to take pleasure in beating her in every exercise we do from now."

"You still need to cool down a bit," I advised. "Healthy competition's one thing – a vendetta's something entirely different."

"The spoiled little witch deserves it," he growled. "But I'm glad you're OK with me, Amy. I love the support of a beautiful girl."

Was he laying it on with a shovel, or what!

I felt myself start to blush and tried to turn away, but Liam put his arms around me and pulled me toward him. It was at that precise, exact moment that Matt came out of the house. He took one look at Liam and me entwined together and his face went white. Without a word he turned on his heel and disappeared back inside.

"You big ape," I shoved hard and broke away. "Now look what you've done!"

"Uh-oh, jealous boyfriend, is he?" Liam seemed to find

the situation funny. "Well, if you ever feel like giving him something to be really jealous about…"

"Oh grow up, jerk." Really annoyed I ran into the house, hoping to find Matt before we saw Darius, but all I got was the door of the lecture room being slammed shut. I yanked it open and hurtled through.

"Hurry up, Amy," Darius was already at the front of the room. "Get yourself a seat."

Flustered, I plunked down in an empty chair, groaning aloud when Liam, following close behind, immediately took the one beside it.

"Go away," I hissed and Darius tapped loudly on his desk with a pointer.

"Quiet, please. I know you won't want to spend more time in here than you have to, so I'll keep it brief and make it quick."

I was very aware of Matt, sitting a couple of rows in front, his head set at a rigid angle as he pointedly ignored me, but, feeling strongly that I hadn't done anything wrong, I concentrated fiercely on Darius.

"This morning was," he chose the word carefully. "Interesting. I have the officials' marks and timings, and I'll go through each one with the student concerned later. As the exercise was run in competition mode I'll give you the placings and a few general comments now."

From the corner of my eye I saw Liam scowl and scuff his boots moodily.

"OK," Darius ran rapidly through his list. "Disqualified, Paris; 5th, Liam; joint 3rd, Kelly and Jack; 2nd, Matt; and 1st, Amy."

The gasp I gave was drowned out by an immediate outburst from Paris. "Disqualified! I rode everything perfectly. You know I did!"

"Your technique was fine, and yes, the score you gained was good, but you rode an incorrect horse on your last discipline. If you'd taken the wrong route on a jumping course you'd expect to be eliminated, so you can't argue."

"Yeah, Paris, and if you'd engage brain before opening mouth for once you'd know that," Liam growled.

"No comments from other students are required," Darius said sternly, and Paris turned in her seat at the front, glaring furiously.

"Yeah, shut up, you!"

"Why should I, you selfish cat? Your stupid mistake cost me the competition. I got so many time faults waiting for you I stood no chance."

"That's enough!" Darius's eyes held the steely glint I'd seen before. "You can all discuss your performance privately with me in a moment. For now, as a group, I'll just say that in general the standard of riding was good, but what the exercise did highlight was the need to stay mentally alert, use all your powers of observation and plan ahead. If you intend to go on to big time competition you'll need all this on a daily basis. It's not only riding skill that's crucial."

I was still shocked at coming in first, and when Darius told us to see him in turns, when he'd go through our performance with the aid of a video recording, I was really excited. He started with Paris, who was still muttering and grumbling about her disqualification, and told the rest of us to wait outside. "You'll be next, Liam, then Jack, Kelly, Matt and Amy.

"Teacher's pet, he's saving you for last because you were

the best," Kelly teased as we flopped down on the grass outside.

"All I can say is the rest of you must have been terrible!" I retorted, laughing. "I lost tons and tons of time and totally messed up the obstacle course. I thought I'd be lucky to come in last!"

"You didn't see me doing that one!" Jack pretended to hold a gun to his temple. "I had Rory, and every time I tried to put the veil on his head he whipped around so I couldn't. It took forever, and in the end we did the course with the veil hanging off one ear."

"Rory gave me a hard time too," Kelly said. "He's fantastic when you get him just right, but he hates too much leg and didn't seem to want to go for me."

I opened my mouth to say I'd found him wonderful, but thought it might come out like I was boasting so I closed it again. I noticed Matt had thrown himself down moodily a few yards away while Liam was still scuffing his feet angrily near the door. I thought they were both acting like spoiled children, and as for Paris – words failed me!

"I wonder if the Barbie Doll is still arguing about her elimination?" Kelly giggled.

"I'm surprised Darius let her off so lightly. He's known for being a real tough teacher," Jack said.

"Maybe he's just setting the rules down at this stage," I suggested. "We've all done plenty of riding training, but his approach is a new one for most of us."

"You mean his use-your-brain-as-well-as-your-body technique?" Jack raised his eyebrows and glanced around at Liam. "There are a couple of idiots here who don't seem particularly blessed in the cerebral department."

"Don't be mean!" Kelly slapped him playfully. "I'm sure Paris and Liam are very smart – just not when they're together, apparently!"

We all giggled at that and tried to straighten our faces as Paris came out of the house. She ignored Liam, who pushed past her on his way back to the lecture hall, but managed a small smile for the three of us.

"It seems I was completely at fault, but there's no way I'm going to apologize to Liam after the way he spoke to me. Well done on winning anyway, Amy."

"Thanks Paris," I said, surprised. "Um – it was hard luck for you mixing up the bay horses."

"No, it was dumb, but I won't do it again, and I certainly won't come in last again. I've never been last in a riding contest before."

"Oh, I have," Jack said cheerfully. "It's character-building, you know."

"Oh *that's* why you've got such a strong character, it's all the losing you do," Kelly whacked him again and they both fell back laughing.

Paris looked confused and I felt sorry for her, the way she just didn't understand goofing around.

"I'm off to study those ponies," she announced. "So that I can become utterly familiarized."

"Don't forget the two in the field, they'll be used as well," I said and she frowned and nodded.

"That's one girl who takes herself far too seriously," Jack said, getting to his feet and brushing himself down. "I'd better get ready for my lecture with Darius, but if he tells me I was awful I'm not going to cut my throat or any-thing."

"Good," Kelly said. "If you did your head might fall off and that would be a shame!"

The two of them were getting very flirtatious, I thought, and felt envious. I'd imagined when Matt and I got together that we'd be getting close and having fun too, but looking over quickly to where he stayed, back firmly turned, it seemed there was no hope at all of that happening.

chapter five

I wanted to explain to Matt about Liam, that *he'd* been the one doing all the cuddling earlier on, but I was scared he'd give me the brush off big time in front of everyone. Anyway, I reasoned, Matt was giving out such mixed signals, 100-watt smiles one minute, cutting me dead the next, that maybe I'd be better off ignoring him too. Watching the sun glint on his thick blonde hair made me feel very regretful, but I was adamant that as I'd done nothing wrong the first move had to come from him. He, unfortunately, didn't see it that way, and the only communication we had was when he called my name brusquely after he came out of the lecture hall.

"Amy. Your turn," he made no eye contact, just left the door open and walked away before I got anywhere near him.

I refused to let it upset me and walked into the big lecture room with a determined smile on my face.

"Well done, Amy," Darius was fiddling around with a screen. "Both at coming first *and* always smiling."

"Maybe the two go together," I suggested, and he laughed.

"Maybe they do, but judging by some of the people I teach I have reason to doubt that! Anyway, take a look at this recording and stop it wherever you've got a question. Meanwhile I'll comment on your performance."

I'd seen myself on film before, but it was nerve-racking watching it with one of the greatest riders in the country. His criticism was very constructive, and he had plenty of good things to say as well.

"The main reason you won is that you took the time to assess each horse. The few minutes you lost calming Shula and Rory down, for instance, were more than made up for by the excellent performance you got from them." He showed me my scores.

"They're good!" I couldn't help sounding surprised. "Apart from the obstacle course. I messed up trying to rush poor Shaft through it."

"Yeah, that wasn't great, but to be fair he's big and clumsy and it was hard luck you got him for that one. That's another thing to bear in mind. You can work your hardest in a contest, and through simple bad luck still lose it."

"Everyone needs a little luck," I agreed, and his austere face broke into a grin.

"And everyone can contribute to their own luck by weighting the odds in their favor – you'll find out more as the course progresses. Did you enjoy this morning?"

"Oh, yeah," I said fervently. "When's the next exercise?"

"You *are* eager," he switched off the screen and my filmed image faded instantly. "This afternoon is more conventional. A group lesson in an outdoor ring followed by 20 minutes in the indoor with individual instruction."

"Are you doing the one-on-one session?" I asked hopefully, and felt a surge of hero-worshipping elation when he nodded. "Oh," I added. "Do we get to choose which horse to ride?"

"No you don't. You keep wanting to choose, Amy. Just who is it you're so attached to?"

"The horse you call Trouble," I grinned at him. "Rory and I are getting along great."

"Well, that's a first. I've never heard anyone say that about him! In fact I'm thinking very seriously of letting him go – despite his undeniable talent he's too unpredictable for the Center. Anyway," his face softened unexpectedly. "I feel sorry for the pony. He hasn't settled here – won't even allow himself to become part of the herd with the other horses! I think he'd be much happier being owned and ridden by just one person."

"I'm sure you're right, I said eagerly. "He's very sensitive, and if he could trust someone and let them get close to him –"

"You really are a fan of his," Darius smiled at my enthusiasm. "Maybe you should be the one to buy him!"

The idea was so powerful, so incredibly wonderful that a big lump developed in my throat and I felt my eyes swim with sudden tears.

Darius, looking horrified, backed off immediately. "Sorry, Amy, don't get carried away. I haven't made a final decision yet, and I'm running a business here, so –"

So Rory, if he were to be sold, would go for a lot of money, is what he meant. It was ridiculous I'd thought for even a moment –

"Yes, of course," I swallowed the lump with difficulty and forced a smile. "I'm not actually in the market to buy a horse, anyway. I'll just enjoy riding him while I'm here."

"And I'll enjoy watching your progress," he looked highly relieved that I'd controlled all that emotion. "See you at the lesson later, then."

Still feeling shaken I tottered from the lecture hall and went to find Kelly and Jack. We had lunch at the house, then an hour or so of comparing notes about the morning's riding, and then it was off to the outdoor ring for our group lesson. This was, as Darius had said, on more conventional lines except that again we swapped horses several times, which really put a new twist on things as we had to adapt to each different mount. I probably found this easier to do than the others, having never owned my own pony. They had mostly worked with just one horse, their own, while my experience had been on a variety of riding school horses over the years. I wondered if the individual lesson with Darius would also consist of changing ponies, so was ecstatic when he called my name first and told me I'd be riding just Rory.

I assumed this selection was also a random one, but I still felt very grateful to Darius for giving my partnership with the bay horse a workout on our own. The lesson was very technical and intense, and I felt absolutely drained by the finish, but the exhaustion was mixed with a great sense of satisfaction. An added bonus of having Rory was that we were now finished for the day and I got to groom, feed and take him back to the paddock. I took twice as long as everyone else in the stables, and when he finally trotted off across his field I went too. He headed purposefully for the far side again, ignoring the other horses that had already settled down nearer the gate to graze.

The first thing he did when he reached his favorite spot was to indulge in a wonderful bout of stress-busting rolling. First he put his head down, sniffing and pawing at the ground, and then he turned around and around before collapsing with a satisfied grunt. I could see him squirm, pushing his back into the grass to get as much contact as possible before balancing on his spine, neatly shod hooves kicking happily above him. He rolled right over, first to one side then the other, repeating the ritual several times and looking so sweet and funny I felt another set of tears prickling away behind my eyes.

"I don't know what's the matter with me, Rory," I rubbed my face fiercely. "I'm not usually an emotional wreck, you know."

The bay horse got to his feet and gave himself a thorough shake before moving forward to nuzzle his soft nose into my neck. It was a very loving gesture, as if to show he was sympathizing with me. I held him gently, feeling the warmth flowing between us. It was a lovely, magical few minutes, but a horse has to do what a horse has to do and soon Rory had settled down to some serious grazing. Still I stayed with him, not hassling or demanding his attention. Just being with him was enough.

I was late getting back for supper. Everyone else was downstairs. I could smell the expensive perfume Paris wore and knew she'd be flaunting yet another designer outfit. I couldn't compete, and anyway I had five minutes to shower and change so, hair still damp and wearing a clean T-shirt, I managed to make it to the dining room just before the food.

"Where've you *been*?" Kelly called out brightly. "We've been back for ages – thought you'd run away with Liam or something!"

I saw a flicker of anger cross Matt's face and I felt irritated at Kelly, but she didn't know how weird Matt was being. We'd already started eating by the time Liam arrived, and would you believe the first thing he did was stroke my hair and say, "Mm, nice."

I jerked my head away but Matt had already turned swiftly, and I felt a knot of annoyance that everything was getting so complicated. Considering Matt wasn't talking to me and Paris and Liam weren't talking to each other, it was a noisy meal, mainly because of Liam who was in outrageous form. He flirted non-stop with me and paid Kelly so many compliments Jack started twitching. He then launched into a really terrible impersonation of Darius telling us all what we were doing wrong in the course so far.

"And now for Liam," Liam was in full clowning mode, exaggerating the slight accent and clipped tones. "If the boy had a brain he'd be a genius. As it is he isn't."

"Well, that's certainly true," Paris swished her long silky hair. "The bit about the no brain, I mean."

"Did anyone hear something?" Liam pretended to look under the table. "I thought there was a kind of high-pitched whining – maybe somebody stepped on a rat."

"Rat yourself," Paris didn't do subtle. "You're not funny Liam, you're pathetic."

"Yup," ignoring her, he made a sudden dive and came up holding one of her exquisite shoes. "That noise is definitely from some sort of vermin – a spoiled brat rodent, I think." He dangled the shoe over a casserole dish on the table. "Oh whoops, nearly dropped it in the food. Wouldn't that be a tragedy?"

"Cut it out, Liam," I said uneasily. "That really isn't funny."

He turned his head and gave me a demonic grin. "It would make me laugh."

"Just stop it," Matt made one swift movement and wrenched the shoe from his hand. "Here you are, Paris."

"Thank you, Matt," she batted her long eyelashes at him.

I saw the muscles in Liam's jaw tighten convulsively, but he sat back in his chair, put his arm around me and leaned over as if to whisper in my ear. I stayed still for a moment, waiting to hear what he'd say, but after making a big deal of nuzzling my hair he didn't say a word. By the time I broke away Matt had left the table and was barging his way out of the room, every inch of his body language shouting frustrated anger.

"Shame. Looks like we upset your boyfriend again," Liam stared across the table. "All we need is for Paris to stomp out of here and life will be pretty much perfect."

"Don't worry," the blonde girl sniffed. "I wouldn't stay in the same room as you if you paid me."

"Wonderful," Liam leaped to his feet and grabbed my hand. "In that case, come on you guys, let's have some fun in the game room."

To say I wasn't eager is putting it mildly, but the alternatives of watching TV with a glowering Matt and Paris or playing third wheel with Kelly and Jack didn't appeal. All four of us wandered over to the big room and had a pool tournament and a few rounds of pinball.

"Here's something different," the hyperactive Liam had found a large box. "Theatrical clothes – we can do a play!"

"No way," Jack said instantly.

"Aw go on. Charades then, or Give-us-a-Clue, whatever you call it."

"How does that work?" Kelly had spotted a glamorous gown.

"Usual old format – one person mimes a book or a film and the rest have to guess it. Only with this box of stuff we get to dress up in character to help the thing along."

"It sounds like a nightmare," Jack was not enthused.

"It'll be funny," Liam grabbed a long blonde wig and a sparkly dress. "Look – old song –" he cavorted about, sticking cushions up the front of the dress and pointing first to the glittering sequins then to his blonde hair.

"I don't get it, you're nuts," Jack said but Kelly, falling down laughing, watched Liam pretend to kiss and cuddle some fake jewelry and gasped, "I know it! It's 'Diamonds are a Girl's Best Friend'!"

"Never heard of it," Jack shook his head grumpily but seemed to warm to the game when Kelly dressed them both up as a cowboy and cowgirl and sat on his lap being all seductive.

I didn't know the name of that one either, but managed to guess a few films later on and even triumphed with a spirited impression of an alien for Star Wars. We made a lot of noise, probably drowning out the TV in the next room, but when we got tired of the game and went in there Paris and Matt had gone.

I was exhausted anyway, and was glad to go back to my room. I leaned out the window and stared at the dark fields where Rory, Fallon, Shula and the others were spending their night. Ragged clouds blew overhead, trailing

60

across the silver disc of the moon so it shone fitfully, only briefly illuminating the group of horses. I tried to pretend I could see Rory, but I knew he'd be removed from the herd, a solitary pony grazing all alone. A great wave of sadness washed over me as I sent him a silent message through the air, a loving goodnight from one lonely heart to another. Was I emotional or what! I think I must have been over-tired.

I slept the minute my head hit the pillow and woke up feeling refreshed and more positive. So, OK, Matt had probably switched his affection to Paris, and Rory was never going to belong to me, but hey! I was at the Caspian Center to learn, not to get a boyfriend or a pony, so that was what I was going to do! There was plenty to concentrate on. Today's schedule was completely different, a morning of lessons ending with a mini competition and an afternoon of fun when we were to take the horses to the nearby coast and swim them in the sea! I live inland and, apart from wading across the odd stream, have never been in the water with a pony, so it was going to be a fantastic first. I hoped and prayed this was one of the times we could choose horses so that I could pick Rory and double/triple/quadruple the thrill. I figured no one else would want him anyway and kept fingers and toes crossed all through breakfast. Fully dressed in riding gear except for my feet I went out to the boot room and found yet another ugly fight going on. As usual Paris was at the center of it.

"But no one *said* I had to clean my own boots. Margo just told us to leave them here before entering the house."

"So did you expect the boots to clean themselves?" Kelly was running out of patience with her.

"I thought Margo or someone would see to it," Paris stuck out her bottom lip in an irritating sulk.

"Don't talk nuts," Kelly pulled on her own shining ones. "You saw me doing mine last night."

"Well you're not me, are you? I'm – I'm –"

"What? More important?" Kelly was being sarcastic, but Paris gave a snooty smile and said, "Yes, exactly. *I'll* never need to do menial work – oh I know, I could pay you to do mine while we're here."

"Get a life, you stuck-up moron," the fiery hair obviously came with a matching temper. "You don't have servants here, so get used to doing some work for a change."

Paris glared at her furiously and they started calling each other some choice names so I grabbed my (clean) boots and escaped outside.

Fed up with everyone, I hung out in the yard, keeping out of their way until Tracey called us together. Again she was holding six head collars and I noticed she was minus glasses and plus lip-gloss. I wondered why until I saw the way she giggled at every joke Liam made and cynically hoped he'd make his over-the-top moves on her rather than me.

"Same start as yesterday," she announced. "Except today Rogan has sore shins so he gets a rest and Rory won't go in the sea, so Darius says you'd better catch Krona or Triest, Amy."

It was a hammer blow, and my disappointment must have shown on my face but I didn't argue. There'd already been enough of that for one morning. I slipped the head collar on Triest, a pretty dapple gray mare, and was leading her toward the gate when Paris's unmistakably shrill voice screeched, "Tracey, Shaft's lost a shoe, look."

The groom moved quickly over to inspect the big horse's right fore hoof. "I'll make a call to the blacksmith." She screwed up her eyes and peered across the field. "You'll have to catch Rory instead, Paris. I think he's way over there."

"Yes, I can see him," the blonde girl said petulantly. "But a) I don't want to walk all that way and get these boots dirty again and b) I heard you say he's really hard to catch."

"Yeah, life's hard sometimes, isn't it?" Tracey said cheerfully. "All I'll say is don't run after him because he'll just keep going, and he's a lot quicker than you."

My every instinct was to step forward and say I'd walk over and get Rory. I hated the thought that Paris might flap and shriek around 'my' sensitive, wary boy – but then I pulled myself up. The blonde girl had already shown what a wonderful rider she was, and there was no reason to think Rory wouldn't cooperate with her now. I stayed quiet and watched her pick her way petulantly across the big paddock. As she got nearer the bay pony he lifted his head and watched her, and then moved away in the slightly insolent manner I'd seen before. Paris didn't run, but she increased her pace slightly and kept on moving toward him. This time Rory waited until she nearly had him, then swished his tail and neatly ducked past her, doubling back to the spot he'd been in before. I saw Paris's shoulders slump and this time, ignoring Tracey's advice, she took a run at him. Rory, showing, along with utter disdain, the sheer class of his movement, flowed instantly into a canter, leaving her floundering way behind him. She tried everything, approaching him cautiously, running at him head on, attempting to cut across his path, even a wild and totally abortive sort of rugby tackle. Rory side-

stepped her every time, moving with a maddeningly graceful air of disdain.

"I can't do it!" her voice rang out across the field, strident and tearful. "He won't let me near him."

"Surprise, surprise," the wicked Tracey murmured mockingly. "Maybe we should leave her without a horse to ride. She'll get another disqualification, but what the heck?"

The others, who seemed to be enjoying the spectacle of Rory making a complete fool of Paris, were in total agreement, but I heard myself say, "No, I'll go and catch Rory. Paris can have Triest."

I felt, positively felt, the eyes of the other students burning into my back as I walked away and knew they were probably thinking I was the biggest creep ever. I don't suppose they'd have believed I was doing this for the pony's sake, not to get into Little-Miss-Rich-Girl's good books, but that was just too bad. I was fed up with the whole group, their moods, quarrels and spitefulness, and I wished with all my heart I could just take Rory and ride off into the sunset.

chapter six

Riding into the sunset with Rory wasn't an option of course,
so, having caught the bay horse by simply walking straight
to him, I made the most of the time spent getting him ready
for his morning's work. He, too, seemed to enjoy our
close contact. He went exceptionally well in the warm-up,
responding instantly to every aid I gave him and moving
with a wonderful lightness and expression. I saw Darius
watching us and felt confident that the picture he was seeing
was one of harmony and balance.

It was a real wrench to dismount and collect Krona, the
chestnut gelding I was to ride in the first lesson. He was
completely different again, a fizzy, bold horse needing
much stronger control. Darius, who seemed to have eyes
in the back of his head, picked up every single mistake we
made, correcting my hands, lower leg and overall position
several times until I'd completely forgotten the earlier glow
of satisfaction I'd enjoyed when riding Rory. Jack was doing

the class on 'my' bay pony and was really struggling. Rory, too well schooled to point-blank refuse, was half-hearted and unenthusiastic, slopping around the school like a disgruntled old nag. Darius, always Mr. Cool, didn't ever shout, but you could hear the frustration in his voice when he tried to correct the pair repeatedly without success. You could see the relief on Jack's face when we got to change horses – he practically leaped off Rory's back and handed him over to Paris.

"Good luck," he said fervently. "You'll need it!"

But in fact, now that she was on his back rather than trying to catch him, the bay horse went well for Paris, responding to her natural balance and the light, positive contact she seemed to know instinctively was right for him. The morning ended with a dressage test followed by a round of jumping.

"It's a combined training contest," Darius told us. "Your score in the dressage plus the timed performance at jumping. You might win one but do badly in the other, in which case you won't get overall first place, so aim for consistency."

As always I hoped desperately to be riding Rory, but instead was given Triest for dressage and Shula for the jumps. I could tell Triest was inclined to be lazy as soon as I moved her forward, but with a lot of strong legwork I got her to produce a pretty creditable test. Waiting to go into the jumping ring I watched Liam hurtling around the course on Fallon, and blinked at the sheer speed and gymnastic prowess they were displaying. Some of Liam's turns were fearlessly tight, but he kept the light bay horse so well balanced he lost none of his momentum and finished with a clear round in what looked to be an unbeatable time.

Shula, the excitable chestnut mare, rose to the challenge beautifully, flying around as though her tail was on fire, and although we tapped a pole at the double it didn't fall, and I was thrilled to go clear as well. I knew it was slower, though. I hadn't taken as many risks as Liam, so I also knew we wouldn't be winning today.

"Still," I told Shula as I patted her extravagantly. "You were great, well done!"

There wasn't much time to do more watching, but from what I did see of the other students they all looked pretty good. We'd dismounted to give the horses a break and were hanging around, not saying much, when Darius came over with the results.

"You're quiet!" he said. "I hoped you'd all be comparing notes."

I didn't want to tell him there were so many issues going on – Matt and me, Paris and Kelly, Paris and Liam, Matt and Liam– that it kind of prevented any easy chat. He must have been aware of the atmosphere but made no comment.

"OK, same system as yesterday. I'll give you the placings now but speak with you individually with your filmed recording later today. The reason I make you do a contest every day is to raise your competitive consciousness, a truly vital component of this game. At the end of your course the results will be combined and the overall winner gets something special. OK, here are today's. 6th, Jack; 5th, Kelly; 4th, Amy; 3rd, Matt."

I could see the knuckles of Liam's hands whiten convulsively.

"2nd, Liam; 1st, Paris," Darius finished rapidly, then gave us a general, dismissive smile and walked away.

"Oh goody," Paris tossed the perfect braid of her hair over her shoulder. "I won."

This was the point at most contests when, even if you're completely disappointed not to have gotten 1st, you crowd around the victor, slap them on the back and say, 'you were great.' Jack and I managed a subdued 'good job' while Matt and Kelly stayed silent, but Liam didn't even bother with basic politeness.

"It's got to be a total fluke! Wait until the cross-country – I'll annihilate you!"

He swung into Krona's saddle and swept away, followed quickly by Kelly and Jack. I saw Matt hesitate, then go over to Paris and say something. He looked awkward and I thought maybe he wanted to hug her or whatever and couldn't with me there, so I hopped swiftly up on Shula and took her back to the yard.

Lunch was a very subdued meal and extremely quiet, as it lacked Liam's constant fooling around. He'd done his stable chores and disappeared, and without him the rest of us didn't seem to have much to say. I'd been looking forward to sharing this whole experience, discussing tactics and comparing performances, but there was none of the friendly banter I'd expected, and of course the closeness I'd hoped would develop between Matt and me was a complete non-starter. He didn't look very happy either; munching his way almost silently through the meal while Paris pointedly ignored Kelly and just threw the occasional remark to Jack and me.

She changed markedly when Liam finally put in an appearance, suddenly pretending to sparkle and blossom. She flirted non-stop with Matt, who looked more puzzled than flattered, laughing at every reply he made as if he was the wittiest person ever. I stamped down a gnawing feeling of jealousy and refused to encourage Liam, who tried some half-hearted flirting with me. I felt a surge of anger that what should have been a wonderful couple of weeks was being ruined by the stupid mind games of these highly talented but ultra-spoiled people. It was a huge, huge relief to get back to what mattered and that, of course, was the riding.

"This afternoon is for fun and relaxation," Darius told us, adding with a straight face, "Judging by your expressions you could all do with some of that, so forget your differences, whatever they are, and enjoy the ride."

Nothing could stop me doing that, I thought, and whistled happily as I got Rory ready. He cocked his intelligent head to one side, listening to the sound with interest and gave me a lovely, friendly nudge with his nose.

"He seems to like you too," Darius was watching from the door. "So I hope you can persuade him to have some fun today."

"Tracey said he doesn't like the sea," I gave the pony a final whisk. "But I'm dead set on having my first horsey swim, so I only hope he realizes that."

"Mm," he didn't sound convinced. "If not, as a reward for all that smiling, you can take Star in. He's so great it's like swimming with dolphins."

"Star?" I looked over to where a dazzling silver-gray Warmblood stood, saddled, bridled and waiting. "Wow! And I could get to ride him?"

"I'd rather see you swim Rory," Darius turned away with a grin, and I led the bay pony out, feeling excitement nibbling at my very toes.

The ride to the coast was beautiful, a winding track through a fragrant meadow into a leafy, rustling thicket of trees where the sun dappled the horses' coats with moving patterns, then a long, gently sloping swath of turf leading to the cliffs. This was the perfect place to gallop, and the hard working horses enjoyed the sensation as much as we did, stretching their necks as their outline lengthened to plunge joyfully into the exhilarating four beat stride. Rory clearly adored the feeling, and again I experienced that wonderful unity, almost as though the horse and I were one being melded together in beauty, power and speed. I could taste the salt tang of the wind in my face and the strength of the pony beneath me, and a wave of pure, untainted happiness engulfed me as I lived and breathed inside that amazing moment.

In the real world Liam, of course, who was riding Baily, was making a race out of it, pushing the super-fast gray so that he forged ahead, leading the other six horses until Darius said in his calm, authoritative way, "Slow it down now, Liam."

I thought for a moment Liam would ignore him or pretend not to hear but, curbing his ultra-competitive nature, he brought Baily down through his paces and we all slowed and then stopped as the track leveled out on the very crest of the cliff. We walked toward the edge and there, below us, lay the ocean, glittering, moving, rolling endlessly, gloriously onto the soft, clean sand of the shore. The track leading down to it was fairly steep, requiring care and patience, and I knew before I was half way down I was in for trouble.

Rory, for the first time with me, was reluctant to move forward, not refusing but resisting, and we took several minutes longer than anyone else to reach the sheltered beach. I decided to let the bay horse take his time, and while the others cantered knee-deep through the waves, sending a million drops of seawater skyward as they splashed and played, Rory and I walked sedately along the edge. The water was a clear azure blue, edged with a ruffle of frothy white and so tempting I ached to be sliding through its silky depths. Rory stopped, dropped his nose and sniffed curiously as the cool shallows swirled around the tips of his toes, and I sat very still giving out positive vibes with every fiber of my being, but leaving the horse to make up his own mind. He did, moving swiftly into reverse to go further back on the shore! I tried riding him along the damp firm sand just above the water's edge, and he was happy to move parallel to the six horses cavorting through the waves, but every time I encouraged him toward the sea he resisted stubbornly.

"Come on, Amy," Kelly, on Shula, was having an absolute ball. "We're going to get their saddles off and take them in for a real swim now."

"Rory doesn't seem to want to." I'd finally persuaded him to get his hooves wet again, but he showed no sign of wanting to go deeper.

I wasn't giving up though, and when everyone else un-tacked their horses and took off riding pants and boots to reveal swimsuits I joined them, relishing the feel of Rory's smooth, muscular back as I vaulted lightly back on. I couldn't help noticing how great Matt looked as he rode Krona confidently back into the sea. Paris quickly joined him, looking like a fabulous mermaid on the dapple gray Triest. Within minutes they were swimming, sliding

72

through the turquoise waves with even sulky Paris laughing
for the sheer joy of the sensation. The other three followed,
with Darius on the big, imposing Star cresting the gentle
swell behind them. The bay pony and I watched, I with
longing and Rory with – what – detachment, disinterest –
fear? He didn't seem afraid, just reluctant, as if he didn't
believe he'd find the experience a pleasant one.

"You'll love it, baby," I crooned, trying to reassure and
make him trust me enough to try. For what seemed like
ages we rode along the very edge of the ocean, looking out
at the six horses swimming joyfully in the deeper reaches
of the bay. I knew it was up to me to persuade the bay pony
to join them, but felt a little hurt that not one of the others
was offering to help until I saw Liam's dark head turn as he
curved Baily through the waves and back toward the shore.

"Here you go Amy, I'll give you a lead. He's bound to
follow, isn't he?"

But no, Rory was having none of it, ignoring all Liam's
best efforts and keeping to his preferred route just above
the water line.

"Amy, you're being way too soft," he turned Baily once
more and splashed determinedly toward us. "It's time to stop
mollycoddling this horse and get him doing what *you* want."

"I don't think –" I began, but Liam didn't do things
halfway. Before I knew it he'd taken a firm grip on Rory's
reins and was urging Baily forward into the water again.

"Kick him on – we're going to *tow* the wicked devil out
to sea!"

Taken by surprise, Rory took several paces forward,
moving rapidly into deeper water, but just as my heart
leaped with excitement the naughty horse stopped dead

74

and jerked his head back hard. Poor Liam, bareback on an already wet and slippery Baily, had no chance of staying put and slid straight off his horse to land spread-eagled on the sea floor with its gentle waves washing right over him! For a horrible moment I thought we'd drowned him, but to my relief he scrambled quickly to his feet, spluttering a lot and calling Rory some of the rudest names I'd ever heard.

Darius, not quite managing to hide the laughter in his voice, called out, "Don't worry, Liam, I'll catch Baily for you," because the gray horse, of course, had simply swum out to re-join his friends.

Liam, only half joking, shook his fist at Rory before plunging back into the sea to scramble onto Baily's sleek, wet back. I knew I should have been very annoyed by Rory's disobedience. It was probably true that I was being too soft with him, but I wanted the horse to *want* to swim and was prepared to wait until he did. I just wished with all my heart I had longer than a few weeks to achieve this. I did manage to get him back to walking hock-deep in the water, and after a few minutes he seemed to relax and start to enjoy it so I felt a minor victory had been won. I even refused Darius's offer to ride Star in the water, feeling very strongly that I wanted my first experience of the sea to be with Rory. Concentrating hard on getting the bay pony to enjoy his paddle, I'd only been vaguely aware of the noise the others were making as they carried on swimming, but a sudden ear-piercingly loud shriek made me look up. Paris, who'd looked even more stunning than usual aboard the shining seal-like Triest had taken a nosedive into the sea. She surfaced with her hair plastered to her skull and seaweed up her nose.

75

"You – you –!" she took in a great gulp of salt water, submerged briefly and came up choking.

"OK, Paris, it's fine, I've got you," Darius calmly swam Star alongside and scooped her up effortlessly. "It's nice to swim beside your pony for a change."

"N- nice!" Still coughing and gasping she scrambled inelegantly back onto her horse. "That – that jerk pulled me in!"

Liam, who, with Matt and Jack, had been swimming alongside the horses, turned a far too innocent face toward her. I couldn't hear what he said but could tell from the maddened shout and angry body language that Paris wasn't impressed. She turned Triest shoreward, plunging through the waves and up onto the beach where she dropped her reins and started messing with her hair.

"Don't let her go, Paris, she'll roll!" I tried to warn her, but the dapple-gray mare had already dropped to the ground and was writhing happily, sending great showers of sand everywhere.

Most of it landed on Paris, whose high-pitched shrieks sent a flock of sleeping seagulls flapping panic-stricken from the rocks. I waited until Triest had finished rolling and had given herself a good shake (sending more great gobs of wet sand all over the blonde girl) and then rode up and grabbed her reins. I handed them to a completely dumbstruck Paris and tried not to laugh at the sight she and the horse now presented. They were both covered in sand from head to foot, face, hair, mane, tail – even their long eyelashes were all plastered in a thick, liberal coating of the gritty stuff. I tried hard not to laugh but Liam, emerging fresh and clean from the sea, didn't bother and almost fell off, he was rocking so much. Even Matt, who could barely raise a smile lately, cracked up, while Kelly and Jack leaned against each other as they laughed.

Darius, like me, made an effort, but his lips were definitely twitching when he said, "It's back in the water I'm afraid, Paris. Dip your head right under and make sure you wash out your pony's ears."

For a moment I thought she would throw the reins at him and burst into tears, but she held it together long enough to march past everyone and lead Triest back into the sea. Even her back view was funny, the glamorous blonde hair hanging like a hank of muddy rope and the small bikini bottoms wrinkled and caked with sand. The others got on with rubbing themselves and the horses with the towels we'd brought while the perfectly dry Rory and I amused ourselves paddling in shallow rock pools.

The sun was warm and the sea breeze lively, so even Paris and Triest were fairly dry by the time we finished our ride back to the Center. The blonde girl hadn't spoken, not one word, on the longer route we'd taken home, and I could see Darius shooting her uneasy glances from time to time. We were to meet up in the lecture hall, he'd told us, once we'd showered and changed, to go through the morning's results.

"Obviously, before you get yourselves fixed up, the horses come first," he said as he dismounted in the yard. "So everyone attend to your own pony and –"

"*Oh* no," Paris slid from Triest's back and handed him the reins. "You can do it, *Mr.* Caspian. I've had it with this place, had it with the bunch of bullies and losers you call students, and I've had it with you! I'm calling my father to take me home, and I'm doing it right now!"

77

chapter seven

For a split second Darius looked shaken, but then he slid smoothly back into Mr. Cool mode. He led both horses over to Tracey, said a few words, and then walked in his usual unhurried way toward the house.

"Now Paris is in for it!" Liam chortled gleefully. "What do you bet Darius throws her out before she gets to tell her dad she quit?"

"Oh give it a rest!" Matt sounded fed up and I supposed miserably it was because, one way or another, the beautiful blonde girl would be leaving.

I didn't want to join in any speculation about what was going to happen, so I quickly led Rory into his stable to untack and groom. The bay horse was, if anything, sweeter and more affectionate than he'd ever been, but I told him sternly it wasn't enough.

"You've *got* to be obedient, you know," I brushed him with long, sweeping strokes. "I know you like me, Rory, so you have to trust me as well. If I ask you to go into the sea you have to do it."

He snorted thoughtfully and gave me his friendly nudge.

"It's no good trying to get around me," I pretended to be mad. "You let me down out there on the beach, and –"

Two sets of footsteps passed the stall door, one heavy and masculine, and the other much lighter. Being nosey I quickly peered outside, just in time to see Paris go into Triest's stable.

"Make sure you get all the salt and sand off," Darius, standing at the door, instructed. "And leave the stable in perfect order. Tracey will be inspecting it later."

I couldn't hear the blonde girl's reply and ducked quickly out of sight while Darius passed Rory's door again. As usual I spent ages with 'my' pony so the yard seemed deserted when I finally led him out. We were strolling contentedly toward the paddock when I heard hoofbeats behind me and turned to see Paris and Triest.

"Hi," I nodded noncommittally but she hurried forward with the dapple-gray pony.

"Amy," her voice was quieter, less shrill than usual.

"Yep?" I tried to keep my own very light.

"Look, I'm sorry about what I said earlier. About – about you all being deadbeats."

"Bullies and losers, I think you called us."

"Oh, well," she ran a hand through her still-sandy hair. "I was mad because when Liam pulled me under the water you all laughed."

"He only yanked you off your horse," I said. "It was just a joke."

"No honestly, he held me down," Paris shot me a sideways look. "It was really scary."

79

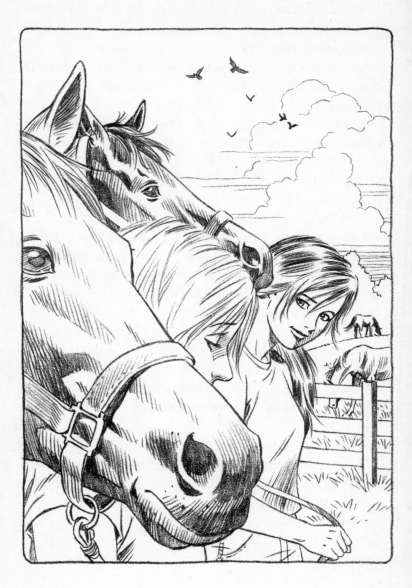

"Not scary enough to justify you leaving," I said bluntly. "I know you're used to having anything you want, but this prize you've won, this course, is worth more than just money. It seems stupid to waste a great opportunity because of some dumb squabble."

She stuck her lip out sulkily but, to my surprise, after a moment's thought, said, "Yeah, that's kind of what Darius told me. I love, really *love* the lessons and the contests, but along with trying to win I'm going to try a lot harder not – not –" she flushed painfully, "not to be such a pain."

"Good," I said sincerely. "I think it's the right decision not to leave."

"Um, well," she fumbled with Triest's head collar. "I couldn't actually get hold of my dad. He's away somewhere, so Darius said since I had to stay I might as well make the most of it."

I wasn't surprised the charismatic Darius had been able to make her stay, more amazed in fact that he still *wanted* her to, and a small part of me couldn't help thinking life at the Center would be a lot pleasanter without her! Still, that was mean of me and I stomped the idea down.

"Are you coming in for supper?" she now asked reservedly.

"In half an hour or so. I want to spend some time out here with Rory first."

"You really are nuts about that pony," she gave me a still tentative smile. "You should get your dad to buy him for you."

I had to bite my tongue to stop myself snapping that, for one I didn't have a dad, and even if I did he might, like most regular dads, not be in a position to buy a high-class horse at the drop of a hat. It seemed to me Paris truly didn't have a clue about real life, so instead I simply shook my head, smiled back (with gritted teeth), and led Rory across the field to his favorite corner. The bay horse and I had a long, interesting chat about our day – yeah I know, I mean I yakked and he ate grass – and I felt that despite the setback of the non-swimming, we were definitely starting to cement the bond between us.

When I went back to the house, however, any sign of bonding between the students was definitely lacking. Liam was in a thunderous mood, not bothering to hide his disappointment at the news that Paris was staying. Kelly told me he'd ranted on for ages, and as soon as the blonde girl appeared downstairs he'd started winding her up again. Arriving, as usual, at the same time as the food, I caught the tail end of a very cruel impersonation of Paris being acted out very loudly by Liam.

"And so I said, ooh Dadsy Wadsy, the nasty teacher disqualified me the first day and then the mean students tried to drown me the next," he'd tied a yellow scarf around his head and was tossing it around the way Paris flung her braid. "And Dadsy Wadsy said, 'Hey kid, didn't you tell me they're all a bunch of losers? You just stay there and wup them good!"

"Do us all a favor and shut up, will you, Liam?" Matt, sitting next to a seriously pouting Paris, looked fed up again. "You're not funny, you know."

"Oh, but he makes me laugh," the blonde girl purred nastily. "I especially like it when he says he's going to win everything and then doesn't. How ya doing so far, Liam? 5th and 2nd, isn't it?"

"You should worry!" Liam's clown face was instantly

replaced by a dark scowl. "What about all the points you lost, getting disqualified for being an idiot?"

"I'll soon make them up," she'd reverted to witch-queen mode. "Let's face it, you group are no competition, so I'll easily win every other class."

"It's not just about winning classes," Kelly was goaded to join in. "We're getting marked on stable management and personal turnout as well."

"Oh, you can come in on top in those if you like. I'm sure you'll do well in a career as a groom," Paris snapped rudely. "Whereas *I'm* going to be a star."

"Some star!" Jack leapt to Kelly's defense. "You'll never get a place in a top team, Paris. Nobody else would want to join it."

"Other stars would," she swung her hair around. "But you'll never know what it's like to be one, so butt out!"

"Paris!" Matt turned in his chair to glare at her. "Calm down and stop antagonizing people."

"You bunch aren't people," she stood up so quickly her chair shot across the room. "You're all future failures giving me a hard time because you're jealous!"

She swept from the room, head high and lips compressed. It was an icily dramatic exit but I was sure I saw her chin quiver and felt an unexpected surge of sympathy.

No one else apparently experienced it.

"Phew!" Jack pretended to mop his brow. "Isn't it great when she stops!"

"She is so – so – *unbearable*," Kelly, also possessed of a hot temper, was still seething. "Telling me I'll never make it as a top rider!"

"She's been driving me nuts," Matt said. "Saying she

83

wants to be 'normal' so everyone will like her. I told her she had to become a lot more reasonable, but as soon as Liam starts making fun of her she lashes out."

"It probably felt like we were all ganging up on her," I said slowly. "She thought we were cruel to laugh this afternoon when Liam dragged her under."

"You make it sound like I tried to drown her," he protested, grinning at me. "I was only joking."

"Princess Paris doesn't *do* jokes," Kelly said spitefully. "She takes everything dead serious and thinks she's the center of the universe."

"Well she's certainly not the center of mine," Jack squeezed her hand meaningfully.

We all started eating, and I have to say it was a much nicer meal without Paris there. Even Matt, who'd seemed closer to her than the rest of us, seemed more able to relax and Liam positively blossomed. He was, once again, all charm and attentiveness, but I remembered the cruel glint in his eyes when he'd laid into Paris and I couldn't shake off the feeling of sympathy for her. She was definitely the worst behaved, most egotistical person I'd ever met, but I was sure it was the result of being spoiled and that she did genuinely want to change. Concerned she was missing out on the meal we'd just enjoyed, I left the dining room and went upstairs, intending to ask her if she'd like something sent up.

As I started approaching her room I saw Darius, his back to me, as he stood outside its closed door. His body language was graphic, the tension showing in his hunched shoulders and bowed head. Paris was obviously still acting up, and I felt sure he wouldn't want me to witness the scene. Acting instinctively, I stepped quickly inside one of the empty bedrooms lining the hallway, just as Margo started to emerge from Paris's room.

"It's no good," I heard her tell Darius. "She won't listen and I can't do anything with her. I suggest we leave her to cool down and I'll try again later."

I stayed, hidden in the dark, listening to their carpet-muffled footsteps coming toward me. I thought they'd just walk by but to my dismay I heard a cell phone ring and Darius stopped just outside the half open door to answer it.

"I'll just take this, Margo," he said, and I saw her smile and nod as she kept on walking.

"Hello," his deep, distinctive voice was cautiously low. "No, no progress at all. Paris is a complete vixen, fights with absolutely everyone and hasn't a single good manner in her pampered body. What? Well, of course in the normal run of things I'd send her packing, but there is the fact that she's easily the most talented rider I've ever seen."

There came a longish pause and I started to think he'd moved on but then I heard him.

"OK, OK, so it's my interest in her father's money that really makes me keep her here. I –" he stopped abruptly and for a horrible moment I thought he'd heard me breathing or something. "Got to go," he said rapidly into the phone and then, to my enormous relief, his footsteps moved swiftly away.

I stayed where I was for several more minutes until I was sure he'd gone, and then cautiously stepped back into the hall. Almost immediately Paris's door opened and her blotchy, tear-stained face looked out.

"Amy, what are you doing?"

I could hardly tell her I'd just been eavesdropping on a conversation about her, so I sighed and went toward her.

"I was coming to see if you wanted anything to eat."

"Oh," for a moment her chin quivered again. "That's nice of you. Darius and Margo brought me a sandwich but I was so mad I threw it at him."

"Oh, right," I said weakly. "Do you want me to get another one?"

This time her whole face trembled and she was half-laughing, half-crying. "You're always so calm and – and normal, Amy. I wish I were like you."

With a penetrating stab I realized that this was probably the very first time the over-indulged, over-confident Paris had ever even considered being someone else.

"Oh well," I was always trying to get her to lighten up. "Normal sandwich it is, then."

In fact Margo, delighted I'd got some response from the sulky, aggressive Paris she'd tried to coax, insisted I take her a nice little tray of salad and a delicious risotto.

"I even brought you dessert," I told Paris, holding up a bar of chocolate. "But only if you'll share."

"I haven't done much sharing," she admitted, picking at a lettuce leaf. "But I guess it's one of the things I should be trying."

"You must be an only child like I am," I sat down on the bed next to her. "My mom says it's harder for kids who grow up automatically getting all the attention. She told me when I was three I had a tantrum when another kid picked up a book I wanted."

"A tantrum? You?" Paris was starting to eat, I was glad to see.

"Apparently. I imagine it was my first and last – I didn't get the book and figured out I was wasting my energy behaving badly about it."

"Behaving badly," she said thoughtfully. "I do a lot of that, but it's always worked – I've never failed to get anything I wanted."

"What about school? You don't get your way there all the time, do you?"

"I'm privately educated," she spoke with a return of her superior manner. "Dad travels a lot and I've always gone with him, so he gets tutors for me."

I couldn't imagine never having experienced school life and all the things that go with it. "But you go to Pony Club? You must, to have won the Caspian prize."

She flushed. "I enter every show my club puts on. I absolutely *love* competition, but not the other stuff."

"You don't do normal meetings? Or go to Camp?" I gaped at her as if she was some kind of alien. "You ought to – they're great and you make tons of friends –" I stopped abruptly, seeing her lower lip tremble.

"Yeah," she brushed a hand fiercely across her eyes. "You guessed it, Amy. I don't have friends, either."

The thought of a weepy, emotional Paris was nearly as scary as the quarrelling, ranting one.

"Hey, well you've got one now," I said hurriedly. "And – er – Matt likes you."

"Yeah, right," she looked at me quizzically. "Look, I'm the dumb one when it comes to relationships, but even I can see Matt's crazy about you and gets jealous when you go off with Liam all the time."

"Go off with –" I stared. "I've never done that!"

"Well, Matt thinks you – doh!" she struck her forehead comically. "He thinks when you disappear before supper you're with Liam, but you're not – you're cuddling that crazy horse you like so much!"

"Rory isn't crazy – how come Matt figures I'm with Liam?"

"Probably because Liam pretends you are," she put down her fork. "I know you all think I overreact to his wind-ups, but that Liam is a real nasty piece of work. I admit I'm selfish, but I don't lie and cheat to get my way."

I couldn't believe Liam did either, but was distracted by a fuzzy warm glow that had started to envelop me.

"Do you really think Matt likes me?" I asked her timidly and she gave me the first genuine smile I'd seen her do.

"He's crazy about you."

Suddenly I was back on Cloud Nine and stayed there until the morning when Matt was waiting for me as I went down the stairs.

"Amy?" He looked sweet, sort of shy but masterful. "I need to talk."

"OK," I said coolly, scared he was going to blow up at me again.

"I thought – I thought you were an item with that creep Liam," the words came out in a rush. "You always seemed to be hugging and flirting, and then I heard him go off with someone that first night, and he said it was you."

"Going off with him? No way!" I said with fervently.

"He's usually late for supper, same as you, and hints you and he have been getting together, but Paris just told me it's not true."

Bless Paris, I thought gratefully, even though I wasn't going to let him off lightly.

88

"You should have checked with me," I said sternly. "Instead of going all moody and giving me the silent treatment."

"I know. I was jealous and scared you'd make a fool of me in front of Liam."

I felt my heart soften like melting ice cream at the anxious expression in his pleading eyes. We spent the next half hour telling each other how we felt and ironing out all the uncomfortable glitches that had come between us. We skipped breakfast, just grabbing a handful of fruit and eating it outside while we lay on the grass talking and laughing in exactly the way I'd longed for. When we finally made a move back toward the house to get ready for the first riding lesson, I thought dreamily that I only needed Rory to develop a lifelong trust in me to make the day perfect. Paris had promised both Matt and me that she was going to make a real effort to rise above Liam's teasing so that she could remain at least civil to the rest of us. Really, I thought the remainder of our stay at the Caspian Center promised to be just idyllic. It was then, as we approached the boot room, that a familiar sound shattered the illusion and brought me crashing back to earth. It was Paris, of course, and she was yelling.

"That's it! How can I be expected to behave rationally when you jerks won't give me a chance? Get my dad on the phone right now – this time I'm definitely leaving!"

chapter eight

"Oh no!" I groaned. What now?"

Matt shrugged. "Someone's probably made Paris break a nail."

"Don't be horrible about her. It was Paris who got us back together, remember."

"I bet that's the first time she's ever done anything for someone else. She's the most self-obsessed person I've ever met," Matt trudged gloomily toward the house, still holding my hand.

"I think she's trying to work on that." The lovely way I was feeling made me want to be kind to everyone. "And the others *do* give her a really hard time. Let's see if we can help."

It was sheer mayhem in the boot room when we reached it. Jack was physically restraining Kelly who, with the light of battle in her green eyes, was trying to reach a still-ranting Paris.

"...pure jealousy and spite from future failures!" The blonde girl spat out the last words and slammed out of the room.

We could hear her yelling Darius's name as she went and my first instinct was to run after her to make her stop.

"Hang on, Amy," Matt put his arm around my shoulder. "Let's find out what's going on."

"It's Paris overreacting and being vile as usual, what else could it be?" Kelly was flushed with anger as Jack cautiously let go of her. "She called us every name she could think of and she knows a *lot*. When's she going to learn to take a joke?"

"I take it Liam's pulled another of his stunts, then?" Matt said and Jack nodded.

I thought I saw a guilty flicker cross Kelly's face and looked straight at her as I asked, "What's he done?"

"Hidden her boots," Kelly said airily. "No big deal."

"I wouldn't say that," the deep voice made us jump; we just hadn't heard Darius approaching. "Destructive and vicious might be more to the point. Do any of you know who did this?"

"Um – not really," Jack said with careful honesty. "I mean, no one saw anybody take the things."

Kelly was staring at Darius. "What are you holding?"

From behind his back he brought the charred, blackened remains of a once-beautiful riding boot. "Only the heel and sole are left of the other one."

There was a stunned silence as we all stared at the burnt, twisted lump of leather.

"Now that's going way too far," Matt looked quite shocked. "He really has got to stop right now."

"He? Who you talking about?" Liam, slouching easily,

91

came into the room and wrinkled his nose. "What's that smell? Someone's barbecue gone wrong?"

Darius held up the remains of the boot, watching him intently. "Someone threw Paris's boots into the furnace."

"No!" Liam stared at all our accusing faces. "Hey, come on guys, if you're thinking I took them – I haven't been near the boot room since yesterday, I promise you."

There was a distinct ring of truth in his words and I saw the muscle in Darius's jaw relax a little.

"A mystery, then."

"None of us would *do* that," Jack muttered.

"The boots didn't walk out of here on their own, did they?" Darius turned toward the door. "Amy, I need to convince Paris that despite this she must stay. Margo has tried to no avail, and says you seem to have a calming effect on the girl. Would you mind coming with me, please?"

"Sure," I followed him silently to the main hallway and up the stairs.

Paris was in her room, wildly flinging armfuls of beautiful clothes into a suitcase.

"I want you to stop that," Darius's voice, as always, had a compelling tone.

"Why?" Paris only paused momentarily. "Everyone hates me, they're going to do everything they can to stop me winning, and winning's the only reason I came here."

"If you leave now then whoever played that nasty trick on you – well, then *they've* won, haven't they?" I stepped forward and gently closed the lid of the suitcase. "Come on Paris, stay here and be a winner."

"I could be," she caught her breath in a sob. "I can do the riding – it's people I don't know how to handle."

"You've just learned your first lesson on how to do that by admitting you have a problem," Darius said. "There's no excuse for the idiot who destroyed your boots, but you have to rise above it and get on with the course. I'll make it clear that any more incidents like this morning will be stomped on hard, but you have to do your bit by not antagonizing everyone."

"I don't know how," she wailed. "I just say what I feel, I always have. I can't help it if Kelly and Jack don't like being told they'll never make the grade and Liam goes mental because I can beat him. I thought it was all right to demand Matt protect me, but he only did it because he hates Liam and now he hates me too. We've only been here for a few days and already they've *all* ended up loathing me."

"I don't," I said bravely. "I like you."

Darius, trying not to look amazed, said heartily, "There you go! There's hope for you yet, Paris."

"I thought I was here to learn how to compete, not how to make friends." At least she wasn't yelling now and she'd made no attempt to re-open the suitcase.

"Competition is about people. I can teach you how to hone your mental and physical approach to riding, but if you can't handle people you're never going to be – what was your ambition?"

"A star," I said, smiling. "Paris wants to be a star."

"Yes I do," she looked very forlorn. "But –"

"But nothing," Darius turned briskly. "Come on, you've got twenty minutes. I want to see you warming up your horse for the first session."

"I can't," Paris said flatly and I took a deep breath,

"Why not?"

"Because I don't have any boots."

It sounded so silly I burst out laughing and, surprisingly, after a startled glance at my face, she actually joined in.

"You mean to say, with all this stuff," Darius waved a hand at the mounds of clothes. "You only brought one pair?"

She nodded. "I thought six pairs of high heels were more important."

"Ah," I jumped up hurriedly, seeing Darius's renowned calm starting to crumble. "I brought an old pair, just in case. They're a half size smaller, so I'll wear them and you can have my others."

"Really? Oh *thanks*, Amy," she looked as if she was going to cry again, so I patted her rapidly, said, "What are friends for?" and rushed off to get the boots.

When we reached the paddock everyone else had already caught a horse and there were only four left.

Tracey, having followed the others to the yard yelled out, "You're late! Shula and Fallon are on rest day so it's Shaft and Rory to come in."

Shaft, the amiable black giant was nearby, but as usual Rory had detached himself and grazed quietly on the far side.

"I'll get him." I thought I ought to run, though my old boots, being a bit tight, made it uncomfortable. The bay pony helped by actually walking toward me, more of a casual saunter than an eager trot, but it still made my heart lift to see him. Hobbling slightly, I led him into the yard and got another boost when Matt bounced out of one of the stables and asked, with obvious concern, if I was OK.

"Sure," I said, stroking Rory's nose. "It's only my boots."

"*Your* boots? I meant are you all right after dealing with the drama queen? Don't tell me someone's damaged your boots as well as hers?"

"No, I loaned them to the drama – I mean Paris. She's going to stay, but she could do with some backup, Matt."

He made a face. "I'd given up, but if you say so I'll try."

To thank him I gave him a quick peck on the cheek and he pretended to faint back against the door, saying, "I'll never wash my face again!"

Grinning, I quickly led Rory into a stall and got him ready. Even if the random selection meant I didn't get to ride the bay horse in the lessons today, being responsible for his preparation meant lots of contact with his grooming and of course at least twenty minutes of mounted warm-up. I thought he was better than ever, supple and responsive and attuned to my every signal. We then followed Tracy, riding a colored cob, through several sets of gates to a kind of undulating valley where Darius, mounted on Star, was waiting.

"Something else to get your brain working on a different track," he said. "This morning you'll all be doing part of this cross-country course," his pointing finger curved in a sweeping arc to encompass the valley spread below. "There are twenty-five varying obstacles throughout the whole course, but I want you to jump just ten of them: the sloping rails, hayrack, arrowhead, wagon, tires, lake, with log in, fence out, hedge and ditch, stone wall, zigzag rails and downhill bank."

I tried hard to look intelligent and hoped we weren't supposed to have memorized that list, because I certainly hadn't.

"Don't worry," he looked at our stunned expressions. "You'll be given the descriptions again and there's nothing you haven't already jumped at some time. There will be officials marking your progress and you will, of course, be timed. Same as usual, but today the difference is," he paused. "*There is no set jumping order*. I want you to ride the course, assess each of the ten jumps, and work out what you consider is the best route in which to take them. Remember to take into account the horse you've been allocated, optimizing his best qualities and making allowances for any possible weaknesses. Any questions?"

I felt like asking, "Can I go home *now*?"

Instead I slapped on a fixed grin and hoped I looked convincing. Despite the daunting prospect no one else spoke either.

"Terrific," there was no trace of irony in Darius's voice. "100% confidence, that's what I like to see. Tracey, hand out the list of fences and the selected horses, please."

I watched the plump, pretty girl handing out first a printed sheet of paper then a narrow strip bearing a horse's name to each of the students in turn. Rory and I were at the end of the line just behind Liam, and as Tracey rode the cob toward us I definitely saw her glance short-sightedly at the last two name slips. Without saying anything she handed one to Liam and the remaining one to me. It was folded in half with the name inside and it said simply, 'Rory.' To say I was ecstatic is putting it mildly. Gratefully, I gave Tracey the biggest grin ever, so that she blushed and quickly turned away.

To begin with, I couldn't think how to tackle the morning's task. I've ridden around quite a few cross-country courses,

96

both on Merrick and riding school ponies, but the route has always been laid out specifically so you know from the start where you're going. Now, as I put Rory into extended canter, feeling the momentum from his hindquarters, I worried that, not only must I correctly identify the required ten jumps but work out from which angle to approach them, calculate the distances between them and decide on a route that would give us the best chance of clearing everything in the shortest possible time.

I could feel my brain hurting at the mere idea, but once I'd found the stone wall and saw that the tires were a straight, slightly uphill gallop away, I started to calm down and really get to work on the project. There were a few fences in the valley that I just didn't know, but mentally ticking off the ten on our list, it wasn't long before I was putting together my plan of action. Rory seemed to be enjoying himself, galloping joyfully when asked, halting obediently to inspect each jump, even appearing to solemnly weigh its approach and take-off point. The only obstacle I could see giving us a problem was the lake. It was a small one, and shallow looking, the jump description merely being 'log into lake, fence out'. The log was slightly elevated but a breeze to jump and there were, I reckoned, only three strides through the water to reach the simple and inviting little fence for the leap back onto dry land. The trouble was, of course, the horse called Trouble was well known for disliking the wet stuff. My experience on the beach had shown me just how reluctant Rory was to go into water so I made the decision to leave the lake until almost last.

"If I make it number nine," I told the bay pony. "You'll

be well into the swing of it and it'll leave us a nice uphill gallop to the arrowhead and then straight on to the finish."

The only other logical plan that I could see was to make the water the second obstacle, but if I did that Rory might well not be fully in the rhythm of the event and could refuse or duck out. I was running out of time for my 'planning phase' but decided to concentrate the last few minutes introducing the tricky pony to the lake.

"Look," I pushed him forward, gently but firmly. "It isn't deep, there's no swimming. I just need you to get your knees wet."

He hesitated, but I wouldn't let him turn away, just kept asking with legs, seat and voice that he move toward the gleaming expanse of water.

"Pretend it's a rock pool," I told him. "We had fun splashing in and out of those."

He seemed to relax and walked more confidently, hardly causing a ripple as he crossed the small lake. I praised him extravagantly, checked my watch and cantered him swiftly up the valley slope to rejoin Darius and the others. Matt was looking for me, and his white teeth flashed in that gorgeous smile as soon as I appeared. Paris, I thought, seemed incredibly focused and constantly referred to her list of jumps. She was riding Krona, the powerful chestnut, who, although a great prospect for cross-country with his bold, fearless outlook, was also very strong and would be a tiring ride. Kelly was on the super-fast Baily, looking suitably terrified at the thought of riding around the valley below on something with virtually no brakes. Matt had the lazy, laid-back Triest, Jack was on Shaft and Liam, giving his impression of the cat that got the cream, had the brilliant, sensitive Rogan.

Darius and Tracey, who'd also been riding through the little valley giving all the fences a last-minute check over, were literally picking names out of a hat, Tracey's riding hat, in fact. The groom's face was screwed up with concentration as she squinted at the bits of paper.

"First to go is Amy," she called, and I felt a whole host of butterflies dance around in my insides.

"You're lucky," Darius gave his rare smile. "Going first means you get to watch all the others. The rest of you must wait on the other side of the gate so you don't get an unfair advantage by watching anyone else's mistakes – or indeed successes."

Matt, who was third in line, rode over and whispered, "Good luck," putting his lips so close to my ear it gave me the shivers.

The shivering seemed to help settle the break-dancing butterflies, and by the time I rode Rory across the starting line I was calm and focused. We reached the stone wall, my first chosen jump, a lot quicker than I'd anticipated and I checked Rory's pace slightly before sitting still and letting him approach it naturally. He lowered his head slightly, lengthening his neck as he measured up the wall and prepared to spring. At the moment of take-off he correctly shortened his neck, raised his head and lifted his forehand. Folding his forelegs neatly, he propelled himself into the air from his hocks, rounding his back and stretching upwards and forwards with all four legs tucked up close to his body. His landing, too, was textbook classic, with straightened forelegs, raised head and supple back. With his hocks well underneath him his getaway stride was perfect and he was already looking ahead to the next jump.

This was a pyramid of tires, and again he cleared it in beautiful, athletic style, wasting no time as we took the curving route to the third choice on my list, the hayrack. From there the valley flattened slightly and the sloping rails, wagon, and a substantial hedge and ditch gave us no trouble at all. The approach to number seven was a long downhill slope, meaning the landing from the bank we had to clear was lower than its take-off, but clever, brilliant Rory soared over with ears pricked. Even when I fumbled slightly with the reins as we maneuvered the zigzag rails he didn't falter, and now we were galloping across a wide, springy expanse of grass to the lake. I knew I must ride positively to fill him with confidence but also realized over-riding would be a mistake. I kept my leg contact positive but very light, knowing how his sensitive skin hated too much pressure.

"Come on, Rory, my precious," I'd used my voice the whole way around, knowing how he liked to hear me, and just hoped the soppy words I'd used hadn't been overheard. "It's just water, nothing to be scared of, I promise you."

Again I felt a slight hesitation, the merest hint that he might be thinking of running away or refusing, but, practically singing encouragement, I maintained his momentum and he cleared the log effortlessly, took three energetic strides across the lake and popped over the fence on the other side. It was a perfect, flawless performance, and best of all Rory seemed to love it! I nearly ruined the whole effect by whooping so loudly and patting him so excessively I nearly fell off, but I pulled myself together and we galloped on triumphantly to our final jump – a well-designed arrowhead that Rory took literally in his stride. Then a flat-out, fabulous run to the finish line and there we were – we'd done it – water and all – we'd done it!

chapter nine

I was so euphoric I couldn't speak, but Darius said later my ear-to-ear grin said it all. He'd ridden Star to an elevated plateau near the finish line where he sat watching intently as each student took his turn in the valley below. I walked Rory around to cool him off, also keeping a sharp eye on the cross-country course as the second to go, Kelly, cantered through the start on Baily. For a moment or two I thought the gray horse was running away with her as he soared into gallop and flew across the course without even looking at a fence, but then I realized she was heading for the lake to make it their first jump. I could kind of see her reasoning. She was hoping to utilize the horse's incredible speed by eating up great swaths of ground, and probably hoped the leap into water would cool and settle him down a little.

Unfortunately Baily didn't see it that way and turned the whole exercise into an overexcited race with no style and hardly any control. Amazingly he managed all the fences, but the course Kelly had decided on meant doubling back on herself to the extent that I thought she might actually jump the tire pyramid twice! I didn't have a stopwatch, but I knew her time was slower than mine, and I'd seen Baily flatten badly at the wagon, sending showers of straw everywhere, which would also mark them down. Kelly had trouble pulling the pony up even after going over the finish line, and by the time she got him back under control and came over to join me, she was deeply despondent.

"What an idiot!" she shook her head in despair. "I'm going to come in last and I deserve it."

I made non-committal, hopefully sympathetic noises and added quickly, "Let's watch Matt. He's just going through the start."

Matt looked fabulous, long-legged, straight-backed, and – and *perfect*. Triest, the dapple mare, was a completely different proposition from speed king Baily, and had to be ridden strongly to get the necessary momentum for the course. Matt did a great job, taking the route I'd have gone for if I hadn't been worried about Rory and the water. He and Triest made the lake their second jump and Kelly, groaning aloud, said, "Oh, that's a much better running order than the one I did. Darius will think I'm a complete idiot."

"No he won't," I said, still walking Rory quietly. I didn't take my eyes off the dapple-gray pony in the valley below. "You'll be fine – oh good *job*, Matt."

All three of us watched Paris, on the ultra-spirited Krona, do an impeccable round, taking the same route as Matt and doing it, I privately admitted, faster and with more style.

"There goes my hope of winning right down the drain," Matt said ruefully. "How come she doesn't have a clue about anything, but can ride a horse that perfectly?"

"You can see why Darius doesn't want her to leave," Kelly said grudgingly. "Looking at her I might just as well give up right now."

"Ridiculous," I said firmly. "We're all here to learn, and we're all potential winners, remember."

"Yeah, right – oh look, there goes Jack!"

Jack, on the enormous, easy-going Shaft, had a wonderful round, choosing a different route, which suited the long stride and big jump of the black horse perfectly. Paris had joined us and I was glad to see she clapped with genuine admiration as Jack galloped Shaft through the finish line way across the valley. She turned away quickly as soon as Liam set off, so didn't see the incredible shortcuts, angles and speed he got from Rogan. I was still on a high from Rory's performance, completely thrilled with his lake jump, so the fact that I knew we weren't going to win the cross-country test wasn't too much of a disappointment. I could see how down Kelly felt, though, and to my surprise Matt looked pretty glum as well.

"You did great," I told him as we rode back to the yard together. "You totally got the best from your horse, and that's what counts."

"What *counts*, as Liam will undoubtedly tell me, is winning," Matt shook his head. "I don't mind getting beaten. I didn't expect to get the best time on Triest, but I'll really, really hate it if Liam comes in first."

"I think Paris could beat him. Her round was flawless."

"Yeah, but she didn't take the risks, cut as many corners

as he did," Matt was unbelievably gloomy. "Nah, Liam's won, and we'll never hear the last of it. He was unbearable enough before."

I privately thought we'd all do better if we concentrated on our own performances rather than whine about anyone else's, but I could see Matt's dislike of Liam ran pretty deep so I stayed quiet.

Once in the stable I was enjoying my usual 'bonding time' with Rory when I heard rapid footsteps approaching, and Paris's graceful blonde head appeared at the door.

"Amy, Darius says he'll give me a lift into town to buy some new boots. Will you come, too?"

I was pleased about the boots, as my old ones were pinching hard, but I'd much rather stay with Rory than shop so I told her so.

Her pretty face fell immediately. "Oh, come on – you said you were my friend!"

"I am, but that doesn't mean I have to do everything you want," I pointed out, reasonably.

She paused. "Please. There's something that involves you– only I can't tell you what it is yet."

Intrigued, I stopped petting the bay pony and walked over to her. "You're only saying that to get your own way."

"No, truly," she looked utterly sincere.

"Oh all right," I came out into the yard. "What about lunch?"

"You can buy a sandwich," Darius had perfected the silent arrival. "We have to go right away so I'm back in time to collate this morning's scores."

"But I need to change!" Paris squealed. "I can't go out in my riding clothes."

"You're buying *riding* boots," Darius pointed out mildly. "So, come on, Paris, take it or leave it. I'm going now."

The blonde girl was still huffing and puffing so I grabbed her arm and towed her off, pushing her unceremoniously into the car. The journey to Cathbay, the nearest town, took twenty minutes or so, and Darius spent the entire time talking to someone on his hands-free cell phone. Paris and I discussed the cross-country course, analyzing every canter, gallop and jump we'd done, and for the first time I thoroughly enjoyed a conversation with her.

"So," she gave me a sly look. "What does everyone say about Darius persuading me to stay?"

I felt a stab of irritation. "No idea. Surprisingly enough, we don't talk about you all the time."

Her face fell. "I suppose not. What about my ruined boots, then? Did anyone admit burning them?"

"No. We – um – we thought it was probably Liam, seeing as you two hate each other so much, but he said definitely not."

"Well he would, wouldn't he?" She thought for a moment. "Actually, I think it was Kelly. She's been mad at me for saying she ought to clean my boots and she looked – I dunno – kind of gleeful when I told her they were gone."

I remembered the guilty look that had crossed Kelly's face and said slowly, "I can't believe she'd be so spiteful."

Paris laughed humorlessly. "Can't you? I'm always coming across stuff like this, so I believe people are capable of anything."

I didn't want to think about the red-haired girl deliberately destroying those beautiful boots so, in my best schoolteacher voice, the one I seemed to be using a lot lately, I said,

"Maybe this sort of thing wouldn't happen if you treated people with respect."

"Respect! What do you mean? I just said –"

"You should stop and think before you speak. *You* might consider you're being honest, but you're actually being plain rude."

"You think?" she was silent for a while, absently rubbing her ankle.

"Does your foot hurt?" Happy to change the subject, I wriggled my own cramped toes. "Both of mine do."

"It's this leather," she flicked the borrowed boots disparagingly. "It's nowhere near as soft as I'm used to."

"There you go again!" I raised my hands in disbelief. "I did you a favor by lending you those and now you're criticizing them. Hasn't anyone ever tried to teach you good manners?"

"No," she said simply. "They haven't."

"Well, wise up, buster!" I was only half-pretending to be mad at her. "Because being a friend is a two-way street, so you have to be good to me as well, you know! You can start by showing some respect, even if the boots I loaned you are a lot cheaper than you're used to."

She was completely silent for several minutes and I thought wearily that she was about to go off on a rant again, but with a visible effort she smiled very sweetly at me. "You're right. I'm sorry. Is that the sort of stuff that makes people hate me?"

"Course it is. Look at you and Liam. All cozy with each other the first night, and then –"

"Hey I'm not taking all the blame when it comes to that guy!" she protested. "I might be irritating, but he's just plain mean. I didn't know what he was like when we were having fun that first night, but I sure wouldn't want him near me now."

I thought about how Matt had heard Liam going off with someone and guessed it must have been her, so I could understand how hurt she must be at the way he treated her now.

"Matt's different," she went on. "He's as cute as Liam, but nice about it. In the beginning he sort of backed me up, but he soon got fed up with me."

"Mm," I wasn't going to tell her Matt's low opinion of her. "He was in kind of a muddle because –"

"Because he thought you'd gone off with Liam and Matt really, *really* likes you," again she gave me a smile with genuine warmth in it and I found myself thinking that with a bit of effort (OK, a massively big effort) Paris could become a very likeable person.

Darius quickly found a parking space in the busy little town of Cathbay and told us we had half an hour before we needed to leave again.

"But I take hours when I shop," Paris wailed, shutting up abruptly when I nudged her hard in the ribs.

I saw the twinkle in Darius's eye and knew he'd noticed, but he merely said, "Thirty minutes, then," and walked briskly away.

Paris had already looked up the address of a shop selling horse gear, so we headed right for it. The price of some of the boots made my scalp tingle and I wasn't surprised when Paris settled on the most expensive pair, but I did admit they were silky soft and quite beautiful. We got some sandwiches and sat in a little park in the center of town to eat them.

"I'm going to wear my new boots," Paris fiddled around while I fed the last of the crumbs to the birds.

"Here are yours," she handed me the store's bag. "Put them on later."

"No, I'll change now – oh, there's Darius – he must be on his way back to the car, so we'd better go."

We rushed from the park (I did a kind of fast limp) and followed Darius, quickly losing sight of him as he turned a corner. Nearing the street where we'd parked, Paris spotted an exclusive looking clothes shop and stared into the window, drooling over a gorgeous white top.

"I gotta have that," she disappeared inside before I could stop her.

"Hurry up!" I yelled at her through the window, stopping suddenly as I caught sight of a familiar face reflected in the glass.

It was Darius, emerging from an alleyway across the road and heading in the direction of the car. Paris came out of the shop looking disgruntled.

"They didn't have it in my size," she complained as I grabbed her arm and hurried her along.

"You've already got a beautiful white sweater, Paris. Come on, Darius will be waiting."

He was standing by the car looking mildly bewildered as he listened to a fat man unsuitably dressed in Bermuda shorts. The man had a map in one hand and was obviously asking for complicated directions. By the time we reached him Bermuda Man had moved away, and we climbed in the car and zoomed back to the Caspian Center. Paris went right upstairs to 'fix her hair' while I gingerly eased my feet out of the too-tight boots.

"Amy!" her voice, though faint, was high and nearly hysterical. I ran in sock-clad feet up the stairs and along the corridor. She was standing in the door of her room and my heart sank when I saw her trembling hands held up to the down-turned line of her mouth.

"What is it?" I joined her quickly and gasped out loud.

The clothes she'd started packing earlier that morning were now thrown in complete disarray around the room. Some, I could see, were badly torn and trampled on, and a whole bottle of perfume had been emptied over a beautiful suede jacket.

"Oh, Paris," the smell of perfume was overpowering and I stepped uncertainly into the room, not knowing where to start cleaning.

"Leave it, Amy," she put a hand on my arm. "I think Darius should see it all first."

We could hear the deep voice coming from his office as we approached it.

"Excuse me," I tapped loudly on the half open door. "Darius, there's been another – incident."

He dealt with everything with his usual efficiency, taking photographs of the mess before it was cleared away, then Margo quietly sorted out the items to be cleaned and those damaged beyond repair. Paris was icy calm but I knew how upset she was and dreaded her meeting the other students. I'm sure Darius felt the same.

"Obviously I have to talk to everyone," he spoke gently to her. "Would you prefer I did it without you present, or –?"

"No, I want to be there," she lifted her chin defiantly. "I haven't done anything to deserve this, so I don't see any reason to hide."

110

"Absolutely not," Darius agreed. "And I must say I'm finding it hard to believe any of your fellow students would behave in this way."

She shrugged. "That's what Amy said, but who else would it be? I guess this latest attack is because I did well in the cross-country earlier."

"But so did everyone else," I put in. "Except maybe Kelly, and she blamed herself, not you."

"I still think the fact that I probably came in first again is enough to send certain people into rage mode," Paris looked straight at Darius. "You must know who I'm talking about. Liam has told us all over and over that he hates, totally hates the thought of being beaten by me."

"You didn't watch him do his round," I said quickly. "You were both clear, but he was definitely faster, and I'm sure he knew it was a winning time."

"True," Darius ran a hand wearily through his dark hair. "Up until now Liam will have been feeling very pleased with himself, with no reason to be vindictive over another defeat by you, Paris."

"Why do you say 'up until now'?" I asked curiously.

Darius sighed and got to his feet. "I knew right away, but Liam was so pleased with himself he didn't notice."

"Notice what?" Paris asked. She was absently stroking the dazzling white sweater, one of the few that had escaped the attack.

"He was so intent on cutting fractions of a second from everywhere that he galloped through the finish at an angle. Rogan went like a dream for him, but the horse actually crossed the line just the wrong side of the marker – so Liam is disqualified."

My first thought wasn't 'oh, what bad luck' or even 'phew, what a jerk' but 'oh no, what's Liam going to do when he finds out?' I didn't have long to wait – we followed Darius out of Paris's room and down to the lecture hall where all six students were being called.

chapter ten

Darius didn't waste any time. As soon as Kelly, Jack, Liam and Matt sat down he told them what had happened. I tried to discern any sign of guilt on the faces of Liam and Kelly, but to me they both looked genuinely shocked.

"With the lack of any other motive, we're assuming one of you four is responsible for these despicable occurrences," Darius said. "We don't know exactly when Paris's boots were put in the furnace but can pinpoint the later attack. Her room was checked by Margo late morning, so the destruction must have taken place between noon and 2:20 when we returned from Cathbay. I'd like you all to tell me where you were between those times."

"First of all," Jack spoke with unusual heat. "I want to tell Paris none of us did any of this."

"That's right," Kelly chimed in. "I know we've had a falling out, Paris, but I'm really sorry your stuff's been damaged, and —"

Darius interrupted, "Thank you both, but right now I'd like you just to tell me where you were."

"Um – it was about noon when we left the yard," Jack frowned in concentration. "We hung out, had some lunch, just chilled, really."

"You were together all the time?"

"I went upstairs once," Kelly stared at us. "But I didn't go near Paris's room, I swear."

"She was only gone a few minutes," Matt offered. "I was in the house too."

"The whole time?" Darius face was a stern, unreadable mask.

"No," Matt paused "I went back to the yard."

"To look for his girl," Liam said lazily. "Worried the lovely Amy was getting cozy with me."

"You said you had a hot date – you implied – " Matt stopped with an effort, a muscle in his cheek working rapidly. "But that has nothing to do with what happened to Paris. I've told you where I was, Darius, but I don't think anyone saw me go to Rory's – I mean the stables, so if you're looking for alibis I don't have one."

"Ah, what a shame," Liam was still winding him up. "Especially as I do. After lunch I met up with Tracey. She had a book she'd promised to lend me."

"The attack on my room probably took less than five minutes," Paris said, her lip curling. "So unless you have a witness for virtually every second you could easily have done it."

"But why would I, Paris my sweet?" Liam bared his teeth in a mock grin. "We all knew you couldn't have beaten my time on the cross country this morning, so no one was going

114

to have to endure your 'I'm wonderful and I've won again' routine."

I saw Darius open his mouth to speak but Paris was quicker.

"I don't talk like that, and anyhow, my sweet, you didn't win. You messed up, cheated again, and you got *disqualified*!"

Liam went very still. "That's not true."

Darius sighed. "I'm afraid it is, though I wouldn't have put it quite like that. You took the finish line at too sharp an angle – Rogan was outside the marker."

Liam growled loudly and moved rapidly across the hall to stand with his back to us at the far side.

Obviously I couldn't see his face, but the tense line of his hunched shoulders and clenched fists gave a clear indication of his feelings. I held my breath, waiting for a further explosion of the temper we'd seen him demonstrate before and found myself exhaling with relief as he turned and walked quietly back to join us.

Darius was also watching him closely. "I'm sorry, Liam. You took one risk too many and I made it clear all competition rules must be adhered to."

"Fair enough," he drew himself up to his full height and looked directly at Paris. "With a disqualification under my belt I really am going to have to win everything else from now on, aren't I?"

She opened her mouth to sneer but Darius said quickly, "That's a good attitude. I want every one of you to be winners, but you have to know how to take defeat as well. Now," he frowned again and I realized suddenly that, despite his constant air of calm, he was actually feeling pretty stressed. "As usual we'll go over your individual performances on the cross-country later. Do you want to know the – er – other placings?"

"Please," Paris had a gleam in her eye.

"OK. 5th Kelly, 4th Matt, 3rd Jack, 2nd Amy, 1st Paris," he reeled off rapidly. "As for the destruction of Paris's belongings, you can be assured I and all my staff will do our utmost to discover who's responsible and will also be extra vigilant to make sure nothing of this nature happens again. You can all cooperate by reporting anything you find suspicious, however trivial and whoever it involves. I know there's been animosity between some of you, and this afternoon's exercise was planned with that in mind, in the hope it will help improve the situation."

"Great," Paris said mockingly. "Have you found a competition where everyone has to like me?"

"We know Darius is good," Liam bared his teeth in a wolf-like snarl at her. "But to achieve that he'd need a miracle!"

"Oh shut –"

"OK, you two, I wasn't sure about this, but you've shown how much you need it. This afternoon's contest is between two teams – Amy, Matt and Jack in one, versus Paris, Liam and Kelly in the other. Your team score will also count in your individual total, so if you decide it's more important to fight with the others on your team rather than accumulate points that's entirely up to you."

There was a short silence.

"Oh, no – what did I do to deserve this?" Poor Kelly looked shell-shocked. "I'll never keep up with Paris and Liam. They'll slaughter me."

"No way," Liam immediately put his arm around her. "We're teammates, all pulling together to beat that old 'B' Team over there."

"Less of the 'B' garbage," Matt shot back. "If we have a name it's going to be 'The Winners'."

There was a lot more fairly good-natured banter, and I was pleased by the lifting of the tense atmosphere at the thought of the new project.

"I wish I was in your team, Amy," Paris seemed the only one who wasn't relishing the idea. "I don't trust Liam one tiny bit."

"He's already said he's trying to get every point he can, so he's not going to ruin his chances by sabotaging you," I said. "And the whole competition takes place under Darius's trained eye, so there can't be any dirty tricks."

"I guess not," she still looked worried, and I gave her a quick hug before we separated to get ready for the contest.

I was still clutching the carrier bag containing the boots she'd borrowed and fumbled in it so I could put them on.

"Oh wow, Matt, look!"

He was walking very close to me and stopped when I did.

I held up a pair of brand new riding boots made of the softest, most supple leather I'd ever seen. "Paris bought me new ones! She can't do that!"

"Sure she can," his blue eyes shone warmly as he looked at me. "You've been good to her, which shows her how *she* should behave. This is probably the first thing she's ever done for anyone else."

"But they're so expensive, I can't take them!"

"You've got to, or she may never try doing another nice

thing in her life. Hey, she can afford it. It's like us buying someone an ice cream cone!"

Genuinely touched, I rushed over and thanked Paris, then wished her good luck, saying, "May the best team win!"

She winked, comically for her. "As long as we don't murder each other, *we* will!"

Running back in the wonderfully comfortable boots I again thought how perfect it all was, but I was deeply disappointed to find our team had been allocated Rogan, Krona and Shaft, while my darling Rory went with Baily and Triest to Paris's team. The competition started with a fairly complicated treasure hunt, with each team member helping each other to solve clues, and then riding through a series of trials and obstacles to fetch required items. The rules, as usual, sounded tortuously complicated, but once we got started it all fell in place and I really enjoyed it. I did some jumping on the talented Rogan, held onto Krona for grim death as we raced back and forth across a shallow stream, and thundered happily over hurdles on easygoing Shaft. Sometimes we were literally riding neck and neck with the opposition, and I was glad to see Rory going really nicely for Paris and even reasonably well for the ultra competitive Liam who adapted his flat-out style to accommodate 'my' pony. With all the hectic relay riding and constant communication between my teammates I didn't see Kelly on him until the very end of the contest.

This part took the form of an elaborate version of an old Pony Club game where a rider gallops to a designated point, collects a marker plus a teammate who vaults onto the horse behind the saddle so that both gallop back to the start. Both riders then jump off and the second one collects another horse to pick up number three member as before. Again both return to the start and jump off, number three gets the last horse and hurtles back to get number one, who's hopefully raced on foot to be in position with the required marker. Simple, eh? Actually, it really isn't that complicated and it's really fun, especially when one of your team's horses is as big as Shaft. Matt, being our tallest, volunteered to do the vaulting onto him and very nearly launched himself into space, having to cling on for dear life with one leg only half over Shaft's rump as Jack thundered back down the track.

From the corner of my eye I could see Rory putting in some very high, disgruntled bucks as Kelly landed with a thump behind Paris. I thought the redheaded girl was sure to come off, but Paris managed to steer the bay pony with one hand while hanging onto Kelly with the other and, with Rory's superior speed, heroically crossed the finish line just ahead of Shaft. We had no idea who'd won over-all, but we were all celebrating surviving the experience, laughing and talking because everyone, even Paris, had enjoyed the event so much. Kelly was still wide eyed at the way Rory had tried to get rid of her.

"I've never known a horse to buck so high! He practically stood on his head, he hated my riding so much! If it wasn't for Paris grabbing hold of me he'd have shot me through the air like a – a *cannon*."

All my sympathies were with Rory, though I realized his behavior wouldn't have pleased Darius who may well have decided that the bay horse really did have to go. I pushed the thought away – it was just too dreadful to contemplate Rory belonging to someone else, and concentrated fiercely

119

on the feeling of euphoria the morning's exercise had brought to us all. Matt was on such a high he picked me up and swung me around, hugging me so tight I could feel his heart beating close to mine.

"Sweet!" Paris was watching, trying to look cynical. "I hope that's not a victory cuddle, because your team only came in second."

"No way, we beat you easily," I wasn't going to let her get away with that and I was genuinely eager to win points even though, like everyone else, I was pretty sure Paris was going to win the course overall. "How did you get along with Liam?"

She shrugged. "OK. He's got talent, but his riding is like everything else about him – too – too –"

"Flamboyant?" " I offered.

"Pain-in-the-neck?" Matt grinned.

"Yeah, that's it," Paris smiled back; her attitude was improving by the hour, it seemed to me.

The result of the team event was, I suppose, a foregone conclusion, but Paris's team only won by a few points so it wasn't going to make much difference to the final outcome. Because we'd had such a good afternoon the evening was much more pleasant too, with both Paris and Liam making an obvious attempt to be civil. Paris wasn't 100% successful, slipping back into her bossy, self-obsessed persona several times, but Liam seemed to be taking the disappointment of the morning's disqualification very well. He stayed resolutely upbeat and ignored the occasional jibe Paris sent his way, and I was impressed. I said so to Paris when we went to get the dress-up clothes for another silly game.

"I don't trust him," she said predictably. "I think it's all an act, and I still think it was Liam who trashed all my stuff."

I couldn't believe that, and just got on with enjoying the fun, particularly the part where Matt and I dressed up as Romeo and Juliet. I blushed so much it felt as though I was about to burst into flames. By eleven we were all wiped out, but before I went to sleep I sent my usual goodnight wishes across the dark fields to the bay pony. It was a peaceful ending to a packed, hectic day and, not surprisingly, I had no trouble falling asleep.

The next morning, after breakfast, all six students had to walk down a twisting, grassy track, skirting one of the fields behind the outdoor ring to a converted barn where we were to watch a farrier's demonstration. Like everyone else I wore my riding stuff, so I'd be ready for whatever lesson we'd be taking the horses through afterwards. I say 'everyone' but in fact Paris, who liked to have an outfit for every occasion, wore jeans (designer of course), with white pointy toe boots and her beautiful zip front white sweater.

"That's too dressy. You're only going to a barn," I pointed out in exasperation, and she tossed her loose, flowing mane of blonde hair petulantly.

"I know the white's a bit much. I'd normally wear a colored top, but the two that aren't trashed are in the wash and my favorite red one is missing."

"No, Paris, I mean you should be in your riding gear. Now you'll have to rush and change when this lecture's over." I gave her a gentle punch in the arm. "Don't be late. I warn you, Darius is strict about timing and he won't wait for anyone."

The talk by the blacksmith was surprisingly interesting

and we were completely absorbed by it for an hour or so. I was particularly interested in the different types of shoes designed to help competition horses, and hung back to ask questions when the others, except Matt, left the barn. Matt didn't have any questions. He was just staying because I did, and I have to say I was really enjoying this 'having a boyfriend' experience. I got good, full explanations to everything I asked, so we had to leave the barn at a run to make sure we'd be on time for our riding lesson. It should have been Rory's day off, but the note on the gate said Krona was slightly lame, meaning he and Baily were being rested, so I joyfully ran over and got my darling boy. Now that everyone knew what each horse was like, it wasn't surprising that Fallon, Rogan and Shula had been chosen, leaving Matt a choice between Shaft and Triest. He picked Shaft, leaving the dapple-gray with the two resting horses.

"Somebody else is really late," Matt led Shaft rapidly toward the yard.

"I hope it's not Paris," I followed with Rory. "She had to get changed and braid her hair, but it shouldn't take that long."

I had a quick check on the three occupied stables, and when I saw Liam, Kelly and Jack, felt a surge of irritation that Paris was taking so long to get ready. My annoyance changed to concern when we all started our warm-up and there was still no sign of her.

"Tracey," I spoke quietly. "Where's Paris? You couldn't go and hurry her up, could you?"

"I'm not allowed to nursemaid any of you," she smiled apologetically. "Liam and I saw her over by the storage barn when we were making our way here, and I said then if she didn't get a move on she'd be late."

"She's going to miss the next contest," I was starting to get really worried. "That means losing points, and she'd never do that."

Tracey shrugged. "She probably couldn't decide what to wear. Don't worry, she's still got a few minutes. Darius went back to his office, so as long as she gets here before he does she'll be all right."

But Darius, when he finally appeared, had no intention of giving the absentee any more leeway.

"Paris not here?" He looked around. "Too bad. It's her specialty, show jumping, today."

I suppose everyone else was thinking that without her they all had a much better chance of winning, but as I cantered into the ring I was sick with worry that only something really bad would keep her away.

chapter eleven

Feeling the way I did, it was hard to concentrate on the tricky course Darius had designed but, as he had constantly reminded us, the rider's brain was his most important asset. I knew this was a challenge I had to meet. Rory was perfect, and with a huge combined effort we achieved a flawless clear round. As soon as we'd finished I went back to worrying about Paris and kept turning around in the hope of seeing her. A lot of time passed. The five of us had been in twice and were now waiting in the warm-up area to start round three, a shorter course against the clock. Liam, riding the superb Fallon, was first to go and the light bay gelding flew around the ring like a beautiful bird, skillfully twisting and turning through the shortest possible route and not touching a thing, not even the lightest tapping of a pole.

"Oh, follow that why don't you, Kelly!" the redheaded girl told herself loudly and I gave her a sympathetic grin – the round was probably unbeatable.

"Amy – Amy!" The cry was faint but unmistakable.

"Paris!" I spun Rory around and took him swiftly in the direction of her voice.

She was still wearing the ridiculous high-heeled boots, trying to run, her hair wild and messy, her T-shirt filthy, the white sweater missing.

"My goodness!" I hurled myself to the ground. "What happened?"

"Someone – someone tried to kidnap me. They locked me in an old storage barn, but I managed to get away – oh, Amy!"

She started to cry helplessly and my heart went out to her. I hugged her, patting her back comfortingly, and when she leaned against Rory he curved his neck around her and gave his gentle nudge.

"OK, what's wrong?" Darius, on Star, galloped up to join us. "Another attack on her room?"

"No." Angry at the lack of sympathy in his voice, I snapped sharply. "An attack on *her*. Someone tried to kidnap her."

"What?" he went sheet white.

Matt, not far behind on the slower Shaft, dismounted immediately and took control, wrapping his own jacket around Paris's trembling shoulders and getting her back to the house. Darius, completely lacking his usual air of authority, rode back to the ring and told the other three the contest was abandoned. Liam's reaction was frightening; I had never seen such naked rage on anyone's face. He screamed abuse, insisting Paris was trying to be the center of attention and had made up the kidnap story as a cover.

"Don't be nuts!" Jack tried to calm him. "Cover for what?"

126

"For not turning up this morning. She was scared I'd beat her, and she was right. My time's unbeatable. Darius, we should finish the class and –"

"For goodness sake," Darius sounded dazed and shocked. "We're not talking about another nasty prank, Liam. Kidnapping is deadly, deadly serious. The police will treat this almost as if it's a murder attempt."

"Police?" Liam quieted down at last.

"Of course. I must phone Paris's father, and he'll want the authorities notified at once, I'm sure."

"It's got to be an outsider," Kelly was very pale. "None of us could possibly –"

"We've been together all morning," I said quickly. "So there's no question of any of us being a suspect."

"That's right," Liam's voice was still surly. "When Tracey and I saw Paris she looked fine, so it must have happened after that."

For once we left Tracey to care for the horses, and all hurried quickly to the house and Paris. Darius seemed to have pulled himself together, and once Margo had made sure Paris had no physical injuries, other than superficial scrapes, he asked her if she could describe exactly what happened.

"I was going back to the house, taking the opposite direction to you guys, I guess, when I saw somebody wave at me over by that scruffy old wooden barn."

"The barn where our old carriages are stored?" Darius said.

She nodded. "The one you can see from my room. I know it sounds weird, but there was just this arm waving a red thing that looked like my best sweater, the one that's missing. I was so mad, and I went over to get it."

127

"Pretty dumb thing to do on your own," I remonstrated.

"Yeah, well I know that *now*, but at the time I thought it was another sick joke, and I wanted to put a stop to it. I stepped inside, but I couldn't see anything – it's really dark in there, with old wheels and stuff piled up high – and then I heard someone behind me. Before I could turn around they kind of grabbed my white sweater and dragged it down around my arms, pinning them to my sides, then they shoved me so hard the sweater came off and they slammed the door on me. I still thought it was Li – one of you – but then I heard these two men's rough, deep voices. One said 'we'll have to move her somewhere safer' and the other one who had a faint accent, growled 'Later. I've got the ransom note – they'll soon know it's her father's money we're after'."

Something horrible pinged in my memory when she repeated those words and I didn't dare speak.

"I'm going to phone your father," Darius said. "He'll want to be here when the police talk to you. Paris, are you sure you didn't see anyone? What about when you escaped?"

She shook her head. "Once I realized no one could hear me screaming I hauled myself up on the old carts and stuff to find a way out. It was hard trying to climb them in the dark. After a while I found a gap at the back of the barn and I managed to wriggle through and lower myself to the ground. I've got no nails left and my fingers bled, look."

In a typical Paris gesture she thrust her once-immaculate hands toward him and I could see they were still trembling. The sight seemed to upset Darius as much as me.

128

"I'm calling your father," he got up abruptly and left the room.

The motherly Margo came back from the kitchen with a hot drink for Paris and continued clucking around and soothing her, so we five students drifted out as well. Liam disappeared immediately, but Jack and Kelly were excited and wanted to discuss the whole thing with us.

"In a minute," I desperately wanted to talk to Matt alone and dragged him away. "Tell me I'm wrong, *please* tell me I'm wrong," I was nearly in tears.

"About what?" He gently pushed the hair away from my face. "What's the matter?"

I took a deep breath. "When Paris told us one of the kidnappers said it was her father's money they were after – well, I've heard those words before!"

"When? By who?"

"That's what's so terrible – it was *Darius* – Darius was speaking on the phone, talking about Paris being difficult and that he wouldn't normally put up with it but he was keeping her here *because of her father's money*."

"But –" Matt looked as shocked as I felt. "He couldn't mean he was going to kidnap her!"

"I didn't take much notice at the time, there was no reason to, but what else could he mean?"

"Uh – maybe he was referring to how much he gets paid to have Paris on this course – no, that can't be right –"

"*None* of us paid for this course – we all, including Paris, won it as a riding prize."

Matt put his arm around me. "And another thing – Paris said one of the kidnappers had a slight accent, just like Darius does. What are we going to do, Amy?"

129

"I don't *know*. I feel for Paris. It was a horrible experience, and though she's been a pain she doesn't deserve any of this, but how can we accuse *Darius*? He's my hero!"

"Mine too. But unless Kelly's right and it's complete outsiders, who else can it be? You can discount the staff, they've all been here for years, unless – what about if Tracey and Liam are working together? She's his alibi again, and says she was with him all the time after they'd seen Paris."

"Tracey's got it bad for Liam, but I'm absolutely sure she wouldn't tell that kind of lie for him. She loves working here and would realize that a kidnapping could be the end of Darius *and* the Caspian Center. But if we're talking about two people covering for each other, what about Kelly and Jack?"

Matt shook his head, "Not Jack. He's the most honest guy I've ever met. Kelly's fiery and she doesn't like Paris, but we're talking *kidnapping*. Anyway, Paris only heard men's voices, didn't she?"

"It's looking worse and worse for Darius," I could hardly bear to say it. "What are we going to *do*, Matt? How can we find out who really did it before the police come and arrest him?"

He looked at me, his eyes very blue and intense. "So you still believe in him? Despite what you heard him say?"

"I know it looks bad," I stuck my chin out. "But, yes, I believe in him."

"We're going to need more than that to convince the police he's innocent," Matt sounded grim. "And Paris's father, of course."

"We need evidence, but I don't know where to look," I

felt frustrated and confused, "I – oh, let's go and check out the storage barn. There might be *something*."

The old wood barn was on the far side of a field that was dotted with trees, its front entrance shielded from view by a thicket of ferns. Matt and I walked all around it, peering at the ground and scanning the weathered boards of the building. There were no windows and the heavy wooden bar locking the door was still in place. I'd been hoping for footprints, but though the thick covering of grass was trampled and worn in places, there were no significant tracks.

"Look," Matt was at the back of the barn, pointing up.

Above him was what had once been a window, now boarded up. The wood there was splintered and broken, the fresh breaks showing clearly.

"That must be Paris's escape route," he looked down at the ground where a few shards of wood were scattered.

"It's quite a drop," I stared up at the narrow gap. "She was pretty brave, forcing her way out of there in the dark, and then hanging by her fingers to get down."

"Totally brave," Matt agreed. "Especially since one of the guys she'd heard could have still been keeping guard outside."

I shuddered at the thought. "So presumably once she was out she took the direct route across the field to find us?"

"Let's walk it," Matt held my hand as he led the way.

A straight line would take us back to the path between house and paddocks, but as we moved along it, something to our right caught my eye.

"There's something over by that tree."

It was Paris's beautiful white sweater, lying in a crumpled

heap beneath a big oak tree. Puzzled, I went to pick it up but Matt stopped me.

"Better leave everything as we find it, Amy."

"Why? Oh – because the police will need to take photos and everything," I bent down and examined the top without touching it. "It's not even grubby, let alone filthy like the other clothes she was wearing. I don't understand what it's doing here, though."

"I guess Paris dropped it on her way," Matt said slowly. "No – that can't be right."

"She said the kidnappers pinned her arms in it at first and sort of yanked it off when they shoved her inside," I looked around us. "So it should really be over by the barn door, not here."

"You think Paris is lying, is that what you're saying?"

"No, but she could be confused, I suppose," I was feeling pretty muddled myself. "Oh look, Matt." I pointed to a long, gleaming blonde hair caught on one of the branches. "She was here, all right, but the white top still doesn't make sense."

We didn't touch the hair and left the sweater lying underneath the tree before going back to the line we thought Paris would have taken.

"Isn't that a heel mark?" Matt, still holding my hand, bent to look at a patch of mud.

"You're right," I peered with him. "There's where her high heel sunk in – you can just make out the pointed toe as well."

"We were right, then. Once she escaped she ran straight across to join the path and get to us." Matt kept on moving slowly across the field, bending every now and then to check for more prints.

Once we were on the path I looked back at the route we'd taken. From here the barn was almost completely hidden in the distance, and I couldn't see the sweater I knew was under the tree.

"That didn't tell us much," Matt echoed my thoughts.

"We'd better go back to the house and tell them about the top. I want to check how Paris said she lost it."

"Good idea," Matt was still open to the idea that Paris might have invented the kidnapping. "We'll see if she changes her story when we tell her where we found it."

The blonde girl, still looking uncharacteristically disheveled, at least had a bit more color in her cheeks now. We told her what we'd been doing, without mentioning the suspicions we had about Darius's behavior, and double-checked her story. She repeated it almost word for word, confirming that the white top had been ripped away from her as she was being forced inside the barn.

"I don't know what it's doing under that tree," she shook her scruffy head. "I probably went that route on the way over, so I could have caught my hair on the tree, but I definitely didn't leave the sweater there."

Kelly and Jack came in with a bunch of wildflowers they'd picked and said nice, supportive things to her. Watching them, I was sure Matt was right, there was no way the honest, considerate Jack would ever do anything underhand or violent, and Kelly's flame-haired temper wasn't teamed with a vindictive nature. Tracey, her plump, pretty face showing concern, also stopped in to see how Paris was doing. Taking her to one side I checked again that she could vouch for Liam, trying hard not to word it quite like that.

"Liam spotted Paris first and pointed her out to me," she looked transparently to be telling the truth. "I did wonder what she was doing way across the field and said she'd be late if she wasn't careful."

"Paris was right over by the storage barn, then? What was she wearing?" I was still concerned about that white top.

"You couldn't miss that white sweater and her hair all loose. She hadn't reached the storage barn. She was by that big oak tree, and I didn't watch to see where she went, sorry – just sort of glimpsed her in passing."

"That's OK, Tracey, thanks. We're just trying to work out where everyone was."

"Yeah, the police will want to know, but it's obvious to me no one from here could have done it."

She patently hadn't considered Darius's absence during the kidnapping period, and I really hoped she'd be proved right. Drearily, I hung around for a while longer, then whispered to Matt that I needed a break and was going to spend some time with Rory.

"Can I come too?" His blue eyes were hopeful, but when I shook my head no he squeezed my hand with understanding.

Instead of taking the short path from the house to the stable yard I decided to take the longer back route overlooking the storage barn field. Deep in thought I walked along the path until I was level with the big oak tree. It was quite a distance, and even when I stopped and screwed my eyes up hard I couldn't see the white top or make out any clear definition of the area surrounding it. The squinting hurt my eyes, and as I rubbed them a sudden thought hit me with

134

devastating clarity. I almost turned back to the house, but needed to think things through before I shared the idea with anyone. If I was right it changed everything and, filled with tension-fueled energy, I found myself running, running hard.

chapter twelve

I ran, of course, straight to Rory. Leaning against him and
breathing in his wonderful, comforting smell, I tried to
make sense of the idea that had flashed into my brain.

"We were sure he couldn't have done it," I told Rory, and
his velvet ears flickered at the sound of my quiet, subdued
voice. "But I can see now –"

I stopped and shook my head. It was an idea, no more, and
the police, when they arrived, wouldn't bother listening to
any half formulated theories. The attempted kidnapping of
Paris Lombard was a serious offence and soon, I was sure,
the Caspian Center would be overrun with trained detectives
searching for evidence, any evidence. I'd have to tell them
about the phone call I'd heard with the comments Darius had
made about being only interested in her father's money, and
the guilty, furtive looks I'd witnessed. They'd soon find out
he'd lied about being in his office during the time Paris was
captured and surely only one conclusion could be drawn.

"We have to face it, Rory," I whispered against the pony's warm shoulder. "I thought Darius was the most wonderful man on earth, and even I can see everything points to him being guilty."

He nudged me gently, then raised his head and gave a little nicker. I heard it too, the brief clatter of hooves of a horse being led from stable to yard. Keeping hidden I peeped over the door just in time to see the rider swing quickly into the saddle, then he and the horse were off, moving rapidly in the direction of the main gate. There was no time to lose and very little to think. I grabbed Rory's bridle and put it on him in one swift movement, buckling his throat lash as I led him from the stable. The other horse, with his fast pace, was already out of sight. I couldn't waste time fitting the saddle, so I led the pony at trot, vaulting onto his bare back as we too speedily left the yard. The center's electronic gate swung open the instant I punched in its code and was already closing when we turned toward the track leading to the coast. I could see the horse and rider way ahead in the meadow; the horse's flanks a pale gleam against the dark backdrop of trees. Not wanting to be seen, I held back, keeping Rory in trot, then a steady canter until we reached the wooded area we'd been through before. I knew as soon as we entered its cool, dappled shade that he was there too. Rory sensed his presence, lifting his sensitive nose and turning liquid brown eyes to scan the leafy glade, and I leaned forward and stroked him, warning him not to call out to the other horse.

We stood very still, listening and watching until the snapping of twigs and a low, muttered exclamation came from somewhere on our right. Soundlessly I moved the bay pony toward the sound, keeping close to a bank of bramble, every muscle tensed and poised for flight. A break in the thicket meant I had a sudden glimpse of him, his dark face creased in a scowl as he looked all around, up into the trees and down to the undergrowth. He was holding something, a plastic bag, crumpled in half, and he seemed to be hunting for a place to hide it. Holding my breath, I leant forward on Rory's smooth back and watched intently through the framework of brambles. Twice he tried stuffing the bag into the crevice of a tree, but then seemed to change his mind, crumpling it further and wedging it under his shirt before pushing his horse onward.

I kept Rory still for as long as I dared, then followed in the same direction, knowing we were now heading for the uphill climb to the coast.

He was galloping, flying like a pale, beautiful bird along the track leading to the cliff top and I followed, feeling horribly exposed and vulnerable out in the open. He was either very confident no one was tracking him or deeply intent on the matter in hand, because he didn't turn once, but just kept the horse going in a fluid, perfect line until they disappeared from view. Rory kept galloping too, every muscle and sinew stretched and rippling beneath me, and despite the frankly scary circumstances I couldn't help reveling in the glorious feeling of power and speed. I'd never ridden so fast without a saddle before, and the by-now familiar feeling of oneness with the wonderful bay pony swept over me in a heady fountain.

I reined Rory in, slowing as we crested the very top of the cliff track, to stare intently ahead for our next glimpse of horse and rider. For a moment I thought we'd lost them.

The sweeping expanse of turf looked empty, and I twisted and turned on Rory's back, searching desperately. Again the pale glimmer of the horse showed me they were way ahead, right up against the slate gray rock at the very edge of the cliff. A single tree and some scrubby vegetation were my only hope of cover, and we managed to reach it in time to see the rider's arm come back as he gazed down at the ocean below him. The bag was in his hand, and as he swung his arm forward I saw him release it, sending it curving in an arc above his head before dropping, down, down to the rocks and the sea. He looked around then, a furtive, sneaking glance, but Rory and I, not moving an inch, stayed hidden, and he quickly turned his head and pushed his horse on, taking the downward, sloping route away from the cliff and out of sight.

This time I didn't wait, putting Rory into canter to reach the point where he'd thrown the mysterious bag. It would be gone, I told myself, already sunk to the bottom of the sea or bobbing far, far out before being submerged and lost forever. I looked down, scanning the jagged rocky cliff side before raising my eyes hopelessly to the surging, restless mass of the ocean. The tide was coming in, and I tried to focus on every wave as it crested against the rocky outcrop directly below. Maybe, just maybe, the plastic bag would be swept, not out to sea, but back to shore – I caught my breath. There, just above the water level, the thing lay, crumpled and folded, on the flat ledge of a rock.

"I see it!" I squeaked in exultation. "We can get it, Rory, whatever it is." It had to be important; I'd already reasoned that, for the rider to bring it out with the sole purpose of hiding or destroying it. "It's *evidence*, that's what it is," I said, and actually had a good idea what the bag contained. "And if anyone's going to believe me, we're going to have to get it."

Rory doesn't actually talk, I know, but his body language spoke volumes. As I urged him toward the rough track leading to the beach below I felt every muscle tense, and he moved without his usual silky rhythm to edge reluctantly downwards. I was considerate and careful with him, of course, but what Liam had referred to as my 'mollycoddling' had to go, and I was much more insistent. As soon as his hooves touched the sand I pushed him on again, seeing the stubborn line of his neck the minute the incoming tide began lapping around his feet.

"Come on, Rory!" I used my legs strongly. "We *have* to do this. We just *have* to!"

At the sound of my voice he relaxed into my hands and allowed me to guide him deeper into the waves, but there was still a long way to go to reach the slab of rock jutting out into the sea. I did everything I'd tried before, but this time, fuelled with urgency, I really, *really* meant it, and to my delight Rory responded, trusting me enough to leave the shallows behind and take the plunge, literally, into the surging ocean. What can I say? I was on a mission, a clue-seeking, vital emergency, but I was doing it on Rory and he was swimming! The sensation was every bit as, well – sensational – as I'd imagined, a fantastic combination of sleek, rippling smoothness and exhilarating motion. Rory loved it too, striking out confidently to cut through the water like an equine powerboat as we headed toward the rocky outcrop. The tide had almost covered the ledge, sending waves crashing and breaking on the gray rock,

their edges curling and lapping against the plastic bag. I had to bring Rory as close as I could, leaning from his slippery wet back, my fingers inching forward to grasp the edge of the bag and pull it safely to me. I'd kicked my lovely new boots off, but my riding pants and T-shirt were soaked, of course, so I jammed the bag firmly under one arm and turned Rory for the swim back to shore.

It was then that I saw him, silhouetted clearly at the top of the cliff, staring down at the beach, the ocean and me. He was already starting to ride down the path, and I thought for one wild moment that Rory and I could turn and swim out to sea, putting as much distance and water as possible between us and the menacing figure on the cliff. I dismissed the idea as quickly as it came, knowing the open ocean was no place for a couple of novice swimmers like Rory and me, and kept going resolutely to the shore. I didn't know what I was going to do when we got there – we could try a galloping escape, but even if we were fast enough we'd soon run out of beach on the curving line of the bay. There was nothing to do but to face the adversary waiting for us on the sand. I patted Rory lovingly as we left the sea, praising him for every single wonderful minute.

"Thought you two couldn't swim," his voice was sneering, his body language threatening.

"We can when it matters," I flicked seawater defiantly in his face. "Which is bad news for you, isn't it?"

"Come on, Amy, give me the bag."

I clamped it more firmly under my arm. "No way. It's evidence."

"You don't even know what's in it. I watched you. You haven't opened it."

"I don't need to," I made my voice deliberately flippant, trying to push down the cold knot of fear in my throat. "I know what's in it."

"No you don't," he leaned suddenly toward me, grabbing for the bag, but I twisted away, almost sliding from Rory's soaked, slippery back.

"Yes I do," I took a deep breath. "It's a red top belonging to Paris and the long blonde wig from the dress-up box."

He swore then, obnoxiously long and hard.

"Shut up, Liam," I knew I was goading him but I couldn't stop. "Your nasty little reign of terror is over. I know you're only sixteen, but how long do you think you'll get for kidnapping?"

"I didn't mean –" he swore again. "I was just trying to get Paris to leave! She wouldn't go no matter what I said or did, so I thought I'd put some serious fright into her. I was only trying to scare her off – there were never any real kidnappers."

"The men's voices were a recording?" I'd guessed that too.

"Yeah, I wanted to get rid of her, that's all. I had no idea Darius would take it seriously and call the police. It was only a – a joke. You know what a pain in the butt Paris is."

"It's not about that, is it?" I had no sympathy for him despite the 'kidnapping' being just one more cruel trick. "It's because she's a great rider and she can beat you at everything she does. Is this what you're going to do for the rest of your life, Liam? Get rid of anyone you think stands in your way? And what about Darius?"

"What do you mean?" his face was dark and petulant.

"I mean in the police's eyes he's going to be suspect

143

number one. When you faked your own alibi didn't it occur to you other people might not have one? No, of course it didn't. You only think about your nasty, selfish self."

"They won't pin this on Darius," he blustered. "Even if they arrest him they'll soon work out the kidnapping was just a fake and they'll let him go."

"Great," I was aware of movement above him. Someone was riding swiftly down the path toward us. "You don't think an arrest for the attempted kidnapping of a student might do his reputation harm? You could have closed the Caspian Center with your stupid, vicious trick and –"

"Shut your mouth!" He lashed out suddenly, knocking me from my precarious seat on Rory's wet back and lunging for the plastic bag as I fell.

The sand was mercifully soft to land on and Rory, bless him, stayed close and nudged me immediately back to my feet.

In a sort of chestnut blur, Shula leaped onto the beach and Matt, looking worried and amazingly wonderful, reined her in and yelled, "Amy! Are you all right?"

"Yes," dripping and sand covered I knew I'd looked better, but the glow in his eyes told me it didn't matter. "Go and get Liam, Matt. He's –"

With a warrior-like roar he drove Shula on, galloping flat-out along the beach in hot pursuit of Liam on the light bay Fallon. It was over pretty quickly, strategy planning obviously not being one of Liam's strong points. Presumably he'd thought he could gallop Fallon right around the bay, but of course he soon found himself cut off by the incoming tide, faced by an almost vertical cliff with nowhere to go. He tried dumping the plastic bag, of course, again hurling it out to sea as far as he could, and I laughed at the frustration he must have felt when it merely bobbed back to shore on the next wave. Matt, looking, even from a distance, extremely powerful and angry, jumped off Shula, hauled Liam off Fallon's back, and retrieved the bag in a couple of easy movements. I could see Liam pleading and groveling and I turned away, concentrating on wiping the worst of the seawater from Rory's coat. By the time I'd washed the sand off myself and forced my damp and gritty feet back into my boots, the two horses had returned. Matt was riding Shula and leading Fallon while Liam, holding his face as if it hurt, trailed miserably on foot behind them.

"What happened to him?" I looked up at Matt.

"He seems to have bumped his head," he said blandly. "What about you? Did he hurt you?"

"Nah," I grinned into his beautiful blue eyes. "I was worried about losing the bag, though."

"No problem," he handed me the scruffy, damp bundle. "Though I don't get it. What was that you said about a blonde wig?"

"Trust me," I patted my darling Rory lovingly. "I'll explain the whole thing!"

✳ ✳ ✳ ✳ ✳

"What I don't see," said Matt much later as he and I were lying on the grass basking in the sun and a lot of reflected glory. "Is how you *thought* of it? What made you realize that although Tracey was under the impression she was telling the truth, Liam had fixed that alibi?"

"I was walking along the bottom path," I waved my hand

145

in its direction, "And I screwed up my eyes to look across at the tree. I realized that's what Tracey does when she's not wearing her specs. She's really shortsighted, and ought to wear her glasses all the time, but she never does when she's near Liam. When he told her Paris was walking across the field she turned and squinted hard and saw –"

"A white top hanging on the tree with the blonde wig above it?" Matt shook his head in disbelief. "She can't possibly have thought she was seeing Paris!"

"I promise you, the girl sees everything as an absolute blur. Liam knows that better than anyone. He started stringing her along with his flirting as soon as he and Paris fell out."

"Do you think he planned it even then? Maybe he hoped Tracey would lie for him, give him an alibi when he needed it?"

"Maybe, but he was wrong there. She'd never be involved with a dirty trick like kidnapping. Liam set it all up himself, and considering he's not too clever it was quite a scam. He used Paris's red top to lure her over, and it was easy for him to shove her inside, making sure he whipped off the white sweater. He locked the door, and while she was in the dark, feeling scared and shocked he played a recording from some old gangster film he watched the other night."

"Nice!" Matt commented. "I bet he wanted to keep her terrified so she wouldn't try to get out in case one of the 'men' was still there."

I nodded. "Paris escaping wasn't in his plan at all. He thought he could win the show jumping before clearing away the evidence. As it was he panicked. The word 'Police' really scared him, so he decided he had to get the

146

red 'decoy' sweater and the wig as far away from the Center as possible. He was still hoping to convince everyone that Paris had invented the whole kidnapping story, so left the white one where it was in the hope we'd doubt her version of what happened. At least that's what I think – he may have just dropped it in sheer panic, of course."

"So how did he set it up? You're saying he played the 'kidnapping' tape, and then ran across and set up his white sweater/blonde wig thing?" Matt still found that hard to believe. "What a sicko!"

"Then he met Tracey and was all flirty walking with her toward the yard. Hardly anyone else uses that path so he was pretty safe, and unless the wig was pointed out to someone with normal eyesight you wouldn't really notice it way over there in the tree."

"But of course he made sure Tracey looked at it."

"Yup. All she saw was a hazy shape of white and blonde, but she genuinely thought it must be Paris, and of course darling Liam, who has perfectly good eyesight, had already said so."

"It's still the most ridiculous thing I ever heard," Matt said.

"Yeah, Darius thought the same," I grinned. "Though Paris said immediately it was just the sort of dumb idea Liam would come up with."

"The frightening thing is he nearly got away with it. What's going to happen to him now?"

"Paris's father has spoken to his father and Liam's being – removed. This isn't the first time he's been in trouble; Margo told me Liam's dad admitted he's been cheating and lying for years, but he's always wheedled his way out of it

147

until now. I think they were too soft – I'd have called the police – but Darius thinks Liam needs psychiatric help more than punishment."

"Mm, it's a shame I didn't know that before I gave him a work over on the beach," Matt said ironically, and we both started giggling.

There was, after all, a lot to laugh about. With Liam gone, life at the Caspian Center was everything I'd hoped it would be and everyone got along really well. I'm not saying Paris was a completely changed person, but she was a whole lot better. She seemed to enjoy having me as a friend and was genuinely grateful I'd solved the whole kidnapping fiasco.

"If you hadn't, my Dad would never have let me go anywhere again," she told me. "He's always been paranoid, so thinking real kidnappers had gotten me would have just about finished him."

I was pretty glad I'd worked it out too. The memory of how it felt worrying that Darius had been involved was truly horrifying. I'd been completely frank and told him about my suspicions. He explained that the phone call I'd overheard was to do with the funding of future prizewinner courses.

"We'd like to get something permanent set up, but we need a sponsor. Mr. Lombard was expressing interest – he said if this year's course benefited Paris we could definitely count on him to put big money into the scheme."

"Then it's a good thing I didn't tell the police what I'd seen and heard," I gulped at the thought. "If Mr. Lombard had found out, you'd be saying goodbye to any funding."

"And probably to my career as well," he admitted.

"Have you broken the news to Tracey?" I asked. "She's going to be upset about Liam turning out to be such a rat."

"She'll get over it," he grinned suddenly. "And maybe it'll cure her of favoring a particular student in the future. I thought Liam reacted uncharacteristically well when I told him he was disqualified, but lovelorn Tracey had already broken the news to him. He also got her to fix it whenever she could so that he wouldn't get Rory, did you realize that?"

"I saw her pick his name and give it to me," I remembered. "But I thought she was being nice to me, not Liam!"

"I'm afraid it's only you who wants Trouble," Darius grinned. "And I'm really looking forward to our next beach trip so I can see the new improved *swimming* Rory!"

The rest of the course was fantastic; we all learned so much, and the competition, though intense, was exhilarating. The overall winner, inevitably, was Paris, but she was pretty cool about it and didn't bait anyone about it, not even the hot-tempered Kelly. Kelly had bravely admitted that she'd been the one who took the blonde girl's boots.

"It really was just a practical joke after the fuss you made about cleaning them. But I promise you all I did was stand them on a mud patch outside – not throw them in the furnace."

"It's OK," Paris said smiling at her. "Liam's already told us he was the one who burned them. My Dad says he's unbalanced, but I think Liam Creedy's just plain bad!"

Matt definitely agreed with her, but I hoped Darius and Mr. Lombard were right and Liam could be helped in some way. Matt and I often saw things from a different viewpoint, but even so we found ourselves getting closer and closer every day and had already promised to see each other regularly once the course was over. Everything was going so well, but the only black cloud on the horizon was, of course, a massively HUGE one. The thought of leaving my darling Rory was totally unbearable, so much so that I was already crying into my pillow at night.

On the very last day, when the final contest was over and we'd done a parade for the Pony Club officials and parents who'd been watching, I slipped away to spend some final precious time alone with the bay pony. He always came to meet me now whenever I walked into his field, and despite his tiring day he still trotted forward, nickering with pleasure. I was sobbing into his strong neck when I felt him raise and turn his head, and I knew someone was coming to join us.

It was Darius, his dark, sensitive face creased with anxiety. "You're not – um – crying, are you, Amy?"

I rubbed my face savagely and looked around at him. "No."

"Good. That's good." For such an articulate and communicative teacher he was hopeless at putting anything emotional into words. "Because," he took a deep breath, obviously deciding a jolly, joking approach would work best, "You don't want to get *your* pony wet."

That almost got me going again and, soggy-eyed, I glared at him angrily.

"Oh no," he reached out and patted my arm gently. "I'm no good at stuff like this. I'll just tell you how it is. Mr. Lombard is completely wowed by the success Paris has achieved and the improvement in her attitude and outlook. He seems to think we've all worked miracles, and has set up the most amazing sponsorship package for future courses."

"Great." I meant it.

"And," he was speaking in a rapid monotone. "Paris has had a lot of input – you know what she's like. This was her idea, but her father and I are in complete agreement. I'm going to get a couple of new horses and move out the less suitable ones – well one, in actual fact."

"You mean Rory?" I stared at him.

"Mm. The course needs horses of varying ability, but although talented, he's just too unpredictable – he won't go at all for some people and that's not really fair."

"It's not his fault!" I burst out. "They just don't understand him!"

"No, but *you* do," his voice became gentle again. "And that's why we, Lombard and I, and especially Paris, want you to have him. Rory needs you too, and I've spoken to your mother and she's fine, and – oh my goodness, you're not going to faint, are you, Amy?"

The next half hour is a complete blank, and I just hope I said all the right things. My mom, who was *totally* blown away by Darius, was fantastic and helped me organize this great arrangement where Rory lives in Uncle George's field but we get the use of Claudia's stable overnight for all the millions and millions of shows we're going to do together. Rory just adores being a one-girl horse and has settled down amazingly. Every day, when I see him grazing happily with his friend Merrick and the other horses, I thank my lucky stars that I now share my life with a horse who *used* to be called Trouble.